SO-AEK-683

BAD NEWS

"Within a few days—or perhaps in a matter of hours—the wings will undoubtedly erupt through the skin. With pressure removed, the pain should no longer be a problem. The wings will be quite fragile, and Ian will have to exercise extreme care. Some arrangement, for example, will have to be made to keep him from rolling onto his back when asleep. Then there's the matter of clothing and . . ."

As Dr. Donovan went on, I cringed on my stool, almost overcome with the horror of what was happening to me.

Afterward, Mom drove me home. Once inside the house, she sank down on the couch, put her face in her hands, and moaned loudly. I ran to my room. I peeled off my shirt, threw myself across my bed, and began bawling.

I was growing wings. I was turning into a freak, like the ones in the circus.

I was also miserable and alone.

For never—not *once*—had either Mom or Dr. Donovan asked me how *I* felt about the ghastly thing that was happening to me.

ALSO BY BILL BRITTAIN

All the Money in the World
Who Knew There'd Be Ghosts?
The Ghost from Beneath the Sea
The Fantastic Freshman
My Buddy, the King
Shape-Changer

———————————

The "Coven Tree" Novels

Devil's Donkey
The Wish Giver
Dr. Dredd's Wagon of Wonders
Professor Popkin's Prodigious Polish

WINGS

A NOVEL BY
BILL BRITTAIN

HarperTrophy
A Division of HarperCollins*Publishers*

Wings
Copyright © 1991 by Bill Brittain
All rights reserved. No part of this book may be used
or reproduced in any manner whatsoever without written
permission except in the case of brief quotations
embodied in critical articles and reviews.
Printed in the United States of America.
For information address
HarperCollins Children's Books,
a division of HarperCollins Publishers,
10 East 53rd Street, New York, NY 10022.

Library of Congress Cataloging-in-Publication Data
Brittain, Bill
    Wings : a novel / by Bill Brittain
        p.   cm.
    Summary: When twelve-year-old Ian grows an unsightly
pair of wings, he becomes an embarrassment to his politically
ambitious father and must look for help from class outcast
Anita and her eccentric mother.
    ISBN 0-06-020648-9. — ISBN 0-06-020649-7 (lib bdg.)
    ISBN 0-06-440612-1 (pbk.)
    [1. Fantasy.]   I. Title.
PZ7.B78067Whe   1991   90-19785
[Fic]—dc20   CIP
                                                          AC

First Harper Trophy edition, 1995.

In memory of Frederic Dannay

1

"How?"

That's the first question I'm asked whenever I'm found out and a snooping reporter or some other busybody begins prying for details.

It's also the one question I don't have an answer for. The doctors, as puzzled as everyone else, have come up with theories like "genetic regression" or "the effects of atomic testing," and maybe they're right. Or perhaps magic does exist in our world, in spite of what the cynics say.

I just don't know.

Since I can't explain *how*, I'll simply tell you about that incredible year . . .

. . . that horrible year . . .

. . . that magnificent year . . .

. . . the year I grew wings.

"Okay, mister. Start talking, or I'll zap you right between the eyes."

"You plug me, cop, and you'll never find out where I hid the diamonds."

"Yeah? Well how about if I just give you a nice friendly pat on the back?"

I lowered my hands and stared in outrage at the plastic squirt gun pointed at my stomach. "No fair, Wayde!" I yelled. "Just because my back's sore, it doesn't mean when we're playing cops 'n robbers you can—"

"Okay, okay." Wayde Flack, my best-friend-in-all-the-world, scuffed his feet on the cement cellar floor and tucked the squirt gun into his belt. "Hey, I didn't mean nothin'."

"This is a dumb game anyway," I grumbled. "Let's do something else."

"Like what?"

We both stared at the tiny basement window high in the wall and listened to the soft brushing of snow hitting the outside glass. "According to the radio, there's an avalanche alert for the whole county," said Wayde. "So I guess skiing's out."

"I couldn't go anyway," I replied. "Dr. Donovan told me I have to rest and take it easy until he finds out what's wrong with my back."

"How long's that gonna take?" Wayde asked.

"It seems like for the past month you've been spending most of your time in ol' Donovan's office."

"It'll take as long as it takes," I said. "I already know I haven't got polio or muscular dystrophy or about a thousand other things. Maybe this afternoon we'll get an answer."

"You're going *again*? Jeez, you were just there, day before yesterday."

"You're beginning to sound like Mom," I told Wayde. "She says taking me to the doctor all these times is lousing up her schedule. Too bad it isn't Diane who's hurting. Mom would sit with her at the doctor's until the world came to an end. But there's nothing wrong with Diane except a serious case of terminal perfection."

"Huh?"

"Diane—Miss Perfect Princess. In school she gets all A's, and she plays all the girls' sports, and she's on the student council, and she was elected freshman prom queen. My parents keep jawing at me about how I ought to be more like her. Jeez, can you imagine me bein' a prom queen?"

Wayde laughed at that. "Big sisters," he replied with a shake of his head. "What a bummer!"

"You said it," I agreed. "The Princess can't do anything wrong. Once when they didn't know I was listening, I heard Dad tell Mom that when Diane came along, they hit the jackpot on the slot machine of children."

"And with you, they figure they got two lemons and a banana, huh?"

"Something like that. I tell them I might like to be an automobile mechanic, and they act like I was planning to spend my life on a street corner with a tin cup. 'Look at Diane,' Mom'll start in. 'Diane already knows how to work the computers down at your father's bank. She wants to make something of herself.' Or 'Someday Diane wants to go into politics, just like your father.' And Diane will do it, too! She'll probably end up being the first woman president of the U.S. I can see it now. She'll be riding around Washington on her white horse—and I'll be walking behind, with a shovel and a broom."

"Speaking of shovels," said Wayde, glancing at the cellar window again, "I heard on the radio that with all this snow, they're having trouble keeping the road through the pass plowed. If it has to be closed, we'll be cut off from civilization." He put a hand to his forehead dramatically and went on in his best British accent. "It's driving me mad, I tell you! Mad, mad, mad!"

"Keep calm, old man," I said, going along with his playacting. "The moment the Blanton grocery runs out of Twinkies, we'll head out over the mountains and across country. We'll see this thing through yet."

"Anyway," said Wayde, reverting to his own voice, "I wish it was April—or May. Then we could climb Chimney Rock or explore one of the old mines or . . . or something."

"As long as we're wishing," I told him, "let's wish for June. School's out in June."

"Yeah. And next year we'll be in eighth grade. No more being the youngest class in high school. You and me, buddy—eighth graders. Think of it."

Wayde poked a playful fist at me. Instinctively I turned to avoid it. The punch—little more than a light tap—landed squarely on my right shoulder blade.

It was as if a great battering ram, tipped with a ball of white-hot steel, had been driven into my back. Agonizing pain lanced up to my shoulder and down my arm and across my ribs. With a loud scream I sank to my knees. Above me, Wayde's eyes grew wide and fearful. "Jeez, Ian," he whispered. "I didn't mean to . . ."

I put my hand into my mouth and bit down hard to muffle any more screams. Then the door at the top of the cellar stairs was yanked open.

"Ian Carras!" I heard Mom call out. "You stop that noise right now. Your father's committee will be arriving any minute for their meeting, and I won't have you howling like a banshee."

"I—I'm sorry, Mom."

"And afterward I've got to make time somehow to get you to Dr. Donovan's office. With all this snow, we'll need to leave early. So Wayde had better go now."

The door slammed shut.

"I'm glad you kept me out of trouble, Ian," said Wayde in a whisper. "But . . . but wasn't she worried that you might be hurt?"

I shook my head. "If it'd been Diane, Mom would have been down here with a first-aid kit under each arm," I told him. "But for me? Well, I guess getting ready for the meeting is more important."

"What meeting?" Wayde asked. "Who has a

meeting when the snow's getting deeper by the minute?"

"Dad's going to run for mayor of Blanton," I said. "He wants to be mayor so bad, he gets the cold sweats just thinking about it."

"But the voting isn't until November. That's nine months away."

"Dad isn't taking any chances. Once he gets his mind made up on a project, he doesn't let anything get in his way. He's already joined every service club in town, so he's only home for dinner about twice a week. And if he plans a meeting, even World War III won't make him cancel it. There's nothing Dad won't do to become mayor."

We gabbed away while Wayde put on his coat and hat and gloves and rubber boots. Finally he left through the outside cellar door. For a long time I just stood there with the door open and snow melting against my face.

The first meeting of the Committee to Elect Lester Carras, which took place in our living room, lasted more than an hour. Toward the end of it, Diane put in an appearance and charmed the socks off all those men and women who'd be helping Dad become mayor.

Me? I was told to stay in my room. But I could hear every word, including Mom's excuse that I was "feeling a little under the weather" and would be seeing the doctor later.

A little under the weather? My shoulders seemed like one huge ache. Aspirin didn't help, either. Mom had given me two of 'em, and I'd sneaked a couple more on my own. As I lay there, trying to ignore the pain, the words I'd said to Wayde Flack kept popping into my mind:

"There's nothing Dad won't do to become mayor."

I knew that was the real reason I was kept away from the meeting. In our family, Diane was Miss Princess.

I was Mr. Also-Ran.

Afterward, when the last of the committee members left to plod home through the deepening snow, Dad and Diane started bundling up in thick winter coats and boots. "Where are you two off to?" Mom asked.

"The bank. If anybody comes in, I'd like to be there to greet 'em personally. And Diane'll show 'em I'm a real family man."

"Anybody who'd come out in this weather just to get to the bank is just plain crazy," said Mom. "I have to get Ian to the doctor. But you . . ."

Dad put his arm about Mom's shoulders. "Crazy people vote too, Madeline," he said. "I mean to win this election and win it big! There's a lot more to Lester Carras than being a small-town banker. Mayor's just the first step. Later on there's the state assembly. Then maybe the U.S. senate. Or even . . ."

I kept hoping he'd at least mention the pain in my shoulders—maybe ask how I was feeling or something like that.

Nothing.

"Ian Carras?" Mrs. Nagel, wearing her starched white nurse's uniform, appeared at the doorway of Dr. Donovan's inner office. "Doctor will see you now. You too, Mrs. Carras."

Mom ushered me ahead of her across the waiting room. Even the gentle brushing of her hand against my back hurt.

The walls of Dr. Donovan's office were covered with plaques and certificates proclaiming his medical skills. Ol' Donovan himself, bald and rather fat, peered over his glasses solemnly. I sat on a small stool so there'd be nothing pressing against my back.

"How are you today, Ian?" Donovan asked with a smile that came and went with the speed of light.

"I'm awful sore," I replied.

"Sit up straight, Ian," Mom ordered. "Don't slouch."

I tried to obey. My back hurt too much.

"Well, Arthur," said Mom, who was on a first-name basis with just about everybody in Blanton, "in the past month, it seems as if we've spent more time here than at home. I hope you've finally found out the cause of Ian's pain."

Dr. Donovan shuffled through papers and X rays in a pair of thick folders on his desk. At the same time he kind of squirmed like he was uneasy about something.

"The patient first complained of severe pains, radiating from the region of the scapulae—the shoulder blades," he muttered finally.

I didn't like being called "the patient."

Dr. Donovan went on. "Two swellings in the upper back were remarkably sensitive to even the slightest pressure. This has been accompanied by a loss of weight—six pounds in the first month alone. As time went on, the swellings grew larger and the weight loss more pronounced—"

"Arthur!" snapped Mom. "Forgive my impatience, but we've been through all this before. Have you found out what's the matter with my son?"

"I—I believe so." Dr. Donovan frowned. His head kept moving back and forth as if somebody'd told him something that was all wrong. He got up, removed four X rays from the folder, and shoved them into place on a large glass display screen. When the screen's light was switched on, there were four pictures of my body, from lower ribs to neck, with all the bones glowing whitely.

"Before I tell you my findings, Madeline, you should know that I've gotten a second opinion about Ian's case."

"Very good, Arthur," said Mom. "And what's the name of the doctor you consulted? We may want to contact him in order to—"

"It wasn't a doctor. It was my son."

"Your son?" Mom's eyebrows shot upward. "But he's a forest ranger, isn't he?"

"Yes. And his preparation for the job included

a number of classes in ornithology."

"Orni— What?"

"Ornithology, Madeline. The study of birds. And I can assure you, my son has been warned never to breathe a word about what we discussed."

Mom looked really scared. "Just . . . just what are you getting at, Arthur?"

"See here." He pointed to the first X ray. "This mass of tissue just at the projection of the shoulder blades."

"I . . . I see it, of course," Mom said. "But what—"

"And here." He indicated another X ray. "This one was taken two weeks later. The mass has gotten considerably larger. It's pressing against the surrounding tissue, which accounts for the pain Ian's experiencing. And the third picture, those filaments of cartilage are changing into shafts of bone."

"Arthur, will you get *on* with it!"

My mother's voice screeched like fingernails scraped across a blackboard. It was one of the few times in my life I had ever seen her lose control. Usually she could remain calm and serene at the longest and most boring of Dad's political meetings, even when her feet were pinched inside tight high-heeled shoes and her girdle was killing her.

"What's the matter with my son?" she demanded.

"In my best medical opinion, Madeline, Ian is growing wings."

There was an awful silence in the office. Mom had a look on her face as if somebody'd dropped a sledgehammer on her head; and I must have looked the same, because Dr. Donovan took a bottle of smelling salts out of a drawer and held it first under Mom's nose and then under mine. Mom staggered to a chair and flopped down in it like somebody'd let the air out of her.

"You—you're joking," she gasped finally.

"I wish that were the case. But I assure you, I've never been more serious."

"Wings? You mean like . . . ?" Mom flapped her hands up and down.

Dr. Donovan nodded. "Incredible as it may seem, that's the only explanation I can offer."

"But how . . . ?"

There it was for the first time—*the question* that would be asked again and again in the weeks and months to come. Dr. Donovan's answer was to shrug his shoulders.

"I just don't know," he told Mom. "There have

been no prior cases anything like this one.
Anatomically, it should be impossible. Humans
don't . . . You see, in birds and other flying verte-
brates—bats, for example—the wings represent
the upper limbs. What in humans are arms and
hands. But in Ian's case, the wings will be an extra
pair of appendages. It's unheard of. Yet it's happening."

"We mustn't allow it to happen," said Mom in
a harsh whisper. Tears were rolling in glittering
streams down her cheeks. "There must be some
kind of an operation—"

"The wings," replied Dr. Donovan, shaking his
head, "appear to be firmly imbedded in Ian's bone
and muscle structure. The operation you're sug-
gesting would have to be performed with great
skill and delicacy or there could be damage to the
rest of his body. Frankly, I'm just not qualified for
such a procedure. However I'd be glad to contact
some surgeons. Perhaps I could locate one who'd
at least be willing to consider—"

"*No you will not!*" Mom's harsh screech rang out
in the small office. "I will not have my son treated
like some kind of a . . . a freak."

"But eventually people are bound to find out."

"Perhaps. But again, perhaps not. I . . . I need time to think about this, Arthur. And to get my husband's opinion. In the meantime, this is our secret. You're not to say a word to anyone!"

Dr. Donovan opened his mouth as if to protest. Then he slowly closed it again. "Very well," he said. "I've made my recommendation, and you choose to ignore it. Have it your own way. But for the good of the boy, I still believe that—"

"Not a word to anyone!" Mom repeated. "Just tell me what's going to happen with Ian's . . . his *wings.*"

"Within a few days—or perhaps in a matter of hours—the wings will undoubtedly erupt through the skin. With pressure removed, the pain should no longer be a problem. The wings will be quite fragile, and Ian will have to exercise extreme care. Some arrangement, for example, will have to be made to keep him from rolling onto his back when asleep. Then there's the matter of clothing and . . ."

As Dr. Donovan went on, I cringed on my stool, almost overcome with the horror of what was happening to me.

Afterward, Mom drove me home. Once inside

the house, she sank down on the couch, put her face in her hands, and moaned loudly. I ran to my room. I peeled off my shirt, threw myself across my bed, and began bawling.

I was growing wings. I was turning into a freak, like the ones in the circus.

I was also miserable and alone.

For never—not *once*—had either Mom or Dr. Donovan asked me how *I* felt about the ghastly thing that was happening to me.

2

For at least an hour I lay there on my stomach, stripped to the waist. I was afraid. I was ashamed. I felt that somehow I was to blame for the awful thing that was happening inside my body.

My stomach seemed to be tying itself into tight knots. My shoulder blades throbbed painfully.

I was turning into something monstrous . . . freakish . . . *different.*

What would Wayde think when the wings appeared? I imagined him laughing at me, while the other seventh graders snickered and tittered.

I thought about running away. But where could I go? The awful wings would mark me as something not quite human, wherever I was.

What could I have done to deserve such a thing? Perhaps I was being punished, just for being born imperfect into such a perfect family.

I wanted to die.

Finally I heard the side door open and close. Dad and Diane were home. There was a babble of voices in the living room as Mom told her "news." Then Dad's voice rang out loudly:

"He's growing *what*?"

I got up, tiptoed to the bedroom door, and opened it a crack.

"You mean like . . . like an angel or something?" I heard Diane ask. "That's disgusting!"

"It's worse," said Dad. "I finally get a crack at being elected mayor, and now this. Heaven only knows what people will think when they find out."

"I'm sure they'll understand, dear," replied Mom, trying to keep her voice from quavering.

"Oh, they'll understand—and they'll pity us," Dad told her. "But in a case like this, pity won't get many votes. They'll want somebody normal down at city hall. And there's nothing normal about having a kid with wings."

I couldn't listen to any more. Pushing the door shut, I sat on the edge of the bed, muffling my sobs with the pillow.

A short while after that there was a knock at the bedroom door. "Ye—yes?" I said, mopping at my damp face with the quilt.

The door opened. Dad came in, carrying a tray. "Mom told me everything," he said grimly. "But wings or no wings, you've got to eat. We thought you'd be more comfortable in here than at the kitchen table."

"But I want to be with you and Mom and—"

Dad shook his head. "As long as you have this . . . this sickness, you'll keep to your own room."

"I'm not sick, Dad."

"Art Donovan says you're growing a pair of wings. Do you call that *normal*?"

"That doesn't mean I'm—"

"I don't know what it means!" Dad roared suddenly.

"Don't yell at me. Please. I can't stand that right now, when I'm feeling so . . . so lousy."

"*You're* feeling lousy?" Dad's voice hammered in my ears. "And just how do you think the rest of us feel, Ian?"

"Dad!" I cried out. "Why don't you just . . . just . . ."

"Just what, Ian Carras?"

"Just shut up! I'm the one who's—"

"You!" He pointed a finger at me like a loaded gun. "You'd tell your own father to shut up? Of all the ungrateful . . . Well, you listen to me, young man. While you live in my house, you'll obey my rules. And I say you keep to your room until we find out what this wings business is going to amount to."

"So I'm a prisoner—is that it?"

"Ah, you'll be fine. You've got TV in here, and books. We'll bring you everything you need. Besides, it'll only be until things get back to normal."

Normal? I wondered whether things would ever be normal again. More than anything, I wanted my father to sit beside me on the bed and just listen while I poured out my fright and grief.

Dad left the room. He closed the door firmly behind him.

All at once my whole body began trembling.

I tried to nibble at some of the macaroni and cheese on the tray. Then my stomach rebelled, and I ran to the bathroom, where I was violently sick.

Midnight came and went. Then one o'clock. Two . . .

It was nearly three in the morning when I finally

dozed off into troubled sleep. Scarcely an hour later I was yanked back to wakefulness by great sheets of pain that made my shoulder blades feel as if they were being twisted in the jaws of giant pincers. I clenched my teeth and groaned as I twisted about on the bed.

Then, as suddenly as it had begun, the pain ceased. It was replaced by a gentle throbbing, strange but not unpleasant, across my upper back. For several minutes I just lay quietly on my stomach, enjoying the first real comfort I'd felt in more than a month.

I flexed my muscles, wondering if the pain would return. No, even the soreness I'd complained of earlier had disappeared. *I'm well again,* I said to myself. Perhaps everything I'd gone through was just a crazy dream and . . .

Then a shudder seized my body as my shoulder blades seemed to *unfold.* It was as if the skin there were like a sheet of crumpled paper that was being flattened. But the sensation did not come from my shoulder blades themselves.

It came from *above* them.

Again I twitched the muscles of my upper back. All the windows in my room were closed tightly.

Still, a soft breeze brushed the hairs of my out-stretched arms.

I flicked on my bedside light, got to my feet, and turned to face the large mirror over my dresser. At first I saw nothing but my own image—twelve-year-old Ian Carras—staring back at me.

Then I turned slightly to one side.

That's when I screamed—again and again and again.

The door to my room banged against the wall as Dad rushed in, followed closely by my mother. Behind them, Diane appeared, still struggling into her quilted bathrobe.

The three of them froze, staring at me as if I were some weird creature from another planet. Mom was the first one to speak.

"I thought at least they'd be soft and feathery," she gasped. "But they're . . . they're . . ."

I looked sidewise at the mirror. The monstrous thing in the glass looked back at me.

Each wing, about the size of a folded newspaper, was supported by a thick shaft of bone that seemed to be an extension of the shoulder blade. The shafts curved outward and upward, coming to points near the base of my neck.

Five long, thin, bony rods hung from the tip of each shaft and gave the wings their shape. This skeleton framework was covered with a membrane of what appeared to be light-brown leather, so thin as to be almost transparent.

Instinctively I twitched my shoulder blades. The wings fluttered loudly in the small room. One of them brushed the wall. A school photograph came loose from its nail and fell to the floor with a crash.

"Oh!" my sister cried out. "They look like . . . like a bat's wings. They're gross!"

It was true. The leathery wings were like those of a giant bat, or some flying reptile long extinct. Yet they were firmly attached to me.

Nearly mad with panic, I flapped the wings to and fro, creating a stiff breeze in my room. "Ian!" Dad shouted. "Stop that at once!"

With an effort of will, I relaxed my muscles. The beating of the wings ceased, and they folded themselves gently against me like two hideous growths covering my back.

"They're so ugly and . . . and ghastly." Mom sank down onto my bed, plunging her face into her hands. "What will we do, Lester?" she moaned. "What will we do?"

"I'll have a talk with Art Donovan." Dad himself was almost in tears. "In the meantime, this whole terrible thing has got to be kept quiet. Not a word to anybody."

"You can depend on me, Daddy," said Diane. "If any of my friends ever see those ugly things, I'll just die!"

"Sleep's out of the question," Dad went on. "So let's go into the living room and make some plans. At least today's Sunday, and the weather's lousy, so nobody's likely to come calling."

I watched Mom and Diane go out into the hall. "Dad," I said, "can I—"

"You stay put!" he snapped. "We wouldn't be in this mess except for you. Now your mother and sister and I have got to figure a way out of it."

He left, closing the door behind him.

I was alone for the next two hours. I spent most of the time standing in front of the mirror and inspecting my new wings. I was both horrified and fascinated by their appearance.

Finally, just as dawn was breaking, Mom came to my room. Her eyes were red and puffy, and she was carrying one of my woolen shirts.

"You can't be going about half naked," she said.

"Even in your room." She tossed the shirt to me. "I've been working with a few odds and ends from my sewing basket. Try it on."

She'd cut two slits up the back of the shirt, from the tail almost to the collar. Each slit was neatly hemmed, and the bottoms were edged with Velcro strips.

I threw the shirt over my shoulders. As I buttoned the front of it, I could feel the back bunch up above my wings.

"Let me help," said Mom as she came up behind me. "You'll have to spread your . . . your wings. And please, Ian, be careful not to touch me with them."

Slowly I extended my wings. I could feel Mom pulling at the woolen cloth until each wing stuck out through a slit. Finally she pressed the Velcro strips into place, closing the shirt's bottom.

"That'll have to do," she said. "It's the only thing I could think of." She put her hand on the doorknob.

"Mom?" I said. "Is Dad still angry at me?"

"He . . . he's just upset, Ian. We all are. The wings—they're like a curse on the whole family. But why? Why us?"

I didn't have an answer. "Can you stay, Mom? Just for a little while? It's lonely in here, and I'm scared, and—"

"You . . . I . . . your father needs me," she replied.

I wanted somehow to make her understand how much *I* needed her just at that moment. But before I could say a word, she scuttled out the bedroom door and was gone.

The days passed, turning into weeks, and March became April. The snow melted, and water poured from the mountains around our small city, turning each tiny creek into a raging river. Early wildflowers began poking up through the muddy earth.

Dad continued his campaign to become mayor. There were, however, no committee meetings at our house. The official excuse was that I had some mysterious sickness that required bed rest and complete peace and quiet.

My books were sent from school, and each day Diane would bring home my assignments and grudgingly assist me in doing the work. One Friday she handed me a gigantic get-well card, signed by everyone in my class. On its front was a ridiculous cartoon of a boy in a hospital bed, his head wrapped in bandages and one leg covered by a huge cast with toes poking out of it. I cried—I was getting pretty good at that—and wished I could swap places with the boy in the bed. He was seriously hurt—but at least he was normal.

I ached with loneliness. I had only my family to talk to, and they spent as little time with me as possible.

The wings themselves grew at an alarming rate until they were like two great leathery sails reaching from the top of my head down to my knees and covering my back like an enormous leathery cape.

It was, of course, impossible for me to sit on any chair with a back. Dad bought me a high stool with a cushion on it. Mom altered several of my shirts as she'd done with the first one, with slits and Velcro fastenings.

I had no problem sleeping. Instinctively I lay on my stomach the whole night, and my wings were never in danger of being crushed. Dad kept the heat on all night so blankets weren't necessary.

Other problems weren't so easy. Baths, of course, were out of the question. The wings made it impossible for me to sit in the tub. Even the shower was a tight fit, and if I forgot and flapped the wings, they banged painfully against the tile.

Sometimes they itched. Scratching required either a yardstick or a coat hanger, bent into whatever shape was necessary.

I had to exercise my wings each day. If I didn't, the muscles that moved them cramped painfully. But each wing, when spread, was the size of a small boat's sail, and flapping them was a real danger to any nearby lamps and vases. So each day I was allowed to go down into our basement, where I beat my wings for half an hour or so.

They made a sound like a tablecloth being shaken out and created great winds in the still air of the cellar, sending dust, cobwebs, and even small bits of wood flying about.

Aside from the daily trip to the basement, I spent almost all the time in my room.

At first I got quite a few telephone calls. Wayde Flack, especially, called three or four times a week. Dad thought it might seem odd for me to be completely cut off from the outside world, so I was allowed to talk on the phone. Wayde would tell me everything that was going on at school and the latest jokes, and we'd make all kinds of plans for new adventures when I was "better."

Dad had made up a story about how I "still felt a little weak" and was "running a low-grade fever," but I felt guilty about lying to Wayde. Whenever he asked too many questions about my being "sick," Mom or Dad would yell for me to hang up, so I knew they always listened in on the extension phone, ready to interrupt if I said anything that might give away the family secret.

Once a week—at ten o'clock in the evening, when the downtown stores had closed and nobody was walking around—Dad drove me to Dr. Donovan's office. It was during one of these visits that I found out about something my father and the doctor were planning for me.

It took a while to get ready. First, Dad draped his black raincoat around me. It was big enough to cover wings and all. Then we went to the garage, where Dad shoved the car's front passenger seat back as far as it would go. I got in and knelt on the seat, facing the rear window. With my wings, this was the only way I could ride.

Dr. Donovan was waiting for us at the side door of his office. We sneaked in like a couple of criminals.

Dr. Donovan examined, weighed, and X-rayed

me. Afterward he sat down for a talk with Dad while I stood in a corner, trying to remember not to flap my wings.

"I'm really worried about Ian's weight loss," Dr. Donovan began. "Twenty pounds already, and there's no end in sight. Is he eating regularly?"

"He gets the same as the rest of us," Dad replied. "And when we bring the plate back from his room, it's always scraped clean."

"His room, Lester?" said Dr. Donovan in surprise. "You have Ian take his meals in his room? But there's no need to isolate the boy. His problem certainly isn't contagious. I'd strongly suggest that you—"

"I'd suggest that you stick to being a doctor and let me handle my family in my own way!" Dad snapped. "Have you found out anything further about the operation?"

Operation? The word was like an alarm bell going off inside my head. What was my father . . . ?

"I'm still looking for just the right surgeon," said Dr. Donovan. "And keeping quiet about those wings doesn't make it any easier. So far, I've been able to present the boy's case as a theoretical problem. Sooner or later, though, I'm going to have to get down to facts."

"Dad?" I whispered hoarsely. "What's this about an operation?"

"How else do you think you're going to get rid of those wings?" he asked over his shoulder.

"But an operation . . . Dad, I'm scared."

"I didn't raise you to be a coward, Ian. And you'll have the best care money can buy. Once everything is set, we'll have those wings cut off and get you back to normal."

With that, Dad turned back to Dr. Donovan. I stared at the rug, mute with terror.

Cut off.

"Remember, Arthur," I heard Dad warn Dr. Donovan, "I won't have Ian's wings becoming the talk of the whole medical profession. Naturally, I want the best person there is. But it's also got to be somebody who won't go blabbing the story around."

"Never fear, Lester," said Dr. Donovan. "I'll see that your secret is kept."

As we left the office, my stomach was churning with panic. Not a word passed between my father and me all the way home.

I really don't believe Dr. Donovan broke his promise to Dad. Maybe Diane—Miss Perfect—made a mistake and said something at school. Or Mom might have allowed a few words to slip out.

However it happened, by the middle of the third week in April, my wings became public knowledge.

3

My room seemed like a prison, and I didn't think I'd ever escape. It became impossible to talk to my father without getting into an argument. I'd say that wings or no wings, I had to get out of the house. Then he'd start in about how I was trying to ruin his political career. Soon we'd be yelling at one another. Each time, Mom would try to make peace between us, but our arguing always ended up with me on my bed, punching my pillow in rage, and Dad pacing through the house and slamming doors. Our biggest battle started with a telephone call one weekend.

From my room, I heard Dad pick up the receiver on the second ring. "Lester Carras speaking."

A pause. Then: "I'm afraid your source—whoever it is—is greatly mistaken, Mr. Bartok."

Another pause.

"Listen, Bartok!" Dad yelled angrily. "You print

one word of that, and I'll sue your socks off. You
and that filthy rag of a paper, both!"

He slammed down the receiver—hard.

"What was that all about, Lester?" Mom asked.

"A newspaper reporter," Dad told her. "Stanley
Bartok, from the Silver City *Sentinel.* Somehow,
he's heard about Ian. He wanted to drive up here
to take some pictures and do an interview."

"What . . . what will we do, Lester?"

"For now, all we can do is sit tight and hope
Bartok will lay off. If word about those wings gets
around, we'll be in a real mess."

Later that afternoon the door chimes bonged.
Mom opened the door as far as the chain lock
would allow. "Yes? What is it?"

"Mrs. Carras?" The man's voice was loud and
shrill. "I'd like to talk to your son. It would only
take a moment and—"

There was a loud thump, followed by a screech
from Mom. "Get your foot out of the door!"

"Ma'am, I'm from *Read-It-Here.* Our newspaper is
sold in grocery stores in all fifty states. We're always on the lookout for stories with a bizarre
slant. And there's a rumor that your son has
grown—"

"Out!" I heard Dad roar. "Go away!"

"Okay. But I'll be back and—" A few more thumps, and then the door slammed shut. I heard both locks click into place.

"They . . . they know, Lester." By the sound of her voice, Mom was close to crying. "How could they have found out?"

"What difference does it make?" said Dad. "The important thing now is what do we do about it?"

"What can we do?"

"We can't keep hiding Ian in the house, that's for sure."

When I heard Dad say those words, I began shaking with excitement. My wings beat the air of the room into a small hurricane. I was going to be *free!*

Then he went on. "We'll have to send Ian away. Someplace where nobody will find him. We can make up a story about how . . ."

I burst out of my room with a loud shout. "No!"

As I scrambled to the doorway to the living room, both Dad and Mom looked up in surprise. "Ian," said Dad, "you shouldn't be in here. Somebody might—"

"I don't care! I can't stand being locked up anymore!"

"Please keep your wings still, dear," said Mom. "It makes me nervous when you flap them that way."

"And stop that yelling, young man," Dad added. "We're your parents, and we don't have to listen—"

"You *do* have to listen!" I shouted. "I want to get out of here and see people and do things."

"Calm down, Ian," said Mom. "Your father was just telling me how we could move you out and—"

"He was talking about hiding me away somewhere else, Mom. But I'm sick of hiding. I want to walk downtown, and play with Wayde Flack, and—and even go to school."

"School?" said Dad. "That's out of the question."

"Why? Because of my wings? I didn't ask for them. I don't want them."

"But you have them," said Dad. "You can't appear in public, looking like . . . like you do now."

"I want to be free!"

"Your mother and I know what's best for you, Ian."

"No you don't. You only know what's best for *you*. All you talk about is how I'm ruining your chance to be mayor. What about me? What about how *I* feel?"

"But dear," said Mom, "you can't go out—to school or anywhere else—until Dr. Donovan finds someone who can—"

"I *will* go to school! Tomorrow!"

"Impossible," said Dad.

"No it's not! If you won't let me go, I'll sneak out a window and . . . and find that reporter and tell him everything that's been going on around here!"

At that, Dad and Mom stared at me in shocked surprise. "You'd never do a thing like that," Dad said.

"Yes I would. I'm going crazy cooped up here."

"The headlines," Dad groaned. "I can see 'em now, Madeline. *Mayoral Candidate Holds Son Prisoner in His Own House.*"

"Lester, you're not thinking of—"

"What else can we do—chain Ian to his bed? If we keep him out of school, he tips off the reporter. Either way, the whole mess is out in the open."

"But school . . . those hideous wings . . ."

"Maybe we can turn 'em into an advantage.

Yeah. We'll send Ian to school. We'll show everybody we're looking after his best interests, no matter what he looks like."

Politics—that was all Dad could think about. But if it would get me back to something like a normal life . . .

"Tomorrow, Dad."

"But Ian," said Mom, "that's so soon."

"What you don't seem to realize, Madeline," said Dad bitterly, "is that whether we like it or not, we've now got to show everyone we're taking this thing in stride. I'll drive Ian down to school and have a little talk with Marty Nesbitt. After all, a principal ought to be able to look after a student in his own building, no matter what the kid looks like."

I'd done it! I'd broken free! But . . .

"I've already alerted Ms. Luskin, Ian's teacher." Mr. Nesbitt, the principal of Blanton Junior-Senior High School, leaned back in his swivel chair and looked across his desk at my father. I stood in a corner. My wings moved lazily to and fro, stirring the warm air of the office.

"She'll inform the other students about Ian's . . .

uh . . . problem," Mr. Nesbitt went on. "But if we get a mob of reporters snooping around . . . well, we're really not prepared for this kind of situation, Lester."

"*You're* not prepared?" replied Dad. "How do you think *I* feel, Marty? I had to sneak Ian out with a coat over him, just to get past that newspaper guy hanging around across the street. If there's any problem, call the police. Chief Hinkley owes me a few favors, so mention my name. Do whatever you have to."

"Well . . . yes, of course. You understand, I'm sure, that we have no way of predicting the reaction of Ian's classmates—and the older students, of course—to . . . to . . ."

"They're wings, Marty. And if just one kid gives my boy any grief because of them, I'll be up here, breathing fire."

"Yes, I'm sure you will. Very well, I told Ms. Luskin we'd be down directly. Shall we go?"

I draped Dad's coat over my folded wings. We left the office and walked along the hallway. "Fortunately," said Mr. Nesbitt, "the seventh and eighth grades are in their own section of the building. And to ease their transition from elementary

school, they're in self-contained classrooms, with
the same teacher all day. Ian should have little or
no contact with the high school students."

We arrived at the door of my room. Through the
small window I could see my classmates laughing
at something Ms. Luskin had said. Mr. Nesbitt
knocked softly.

Ms. Luskin opened the door, looked down at
me, and smiled. In the past weeks I hadn't seen
many smiles. I grinned shyly back at her.

"Come in, Ian," she said. "It's good to have you
back."

I walked into the room. Dad started to come in
behind me, but Ms. Luskin held up a hand like a
traffic cop. "Here, Ian's my responsibility, Mr.
Carras," she said. "You'd best get back to your
bank."

Dad started to protest, but Mr. Nesbitt poked
him gently with an elbow. "Ms. Luskin knows her
business," he said. "Trust her, Lester."

Dad backed away. Ms. Luskin closed the door.
There I stood, with the big coat hiding my wings,
in front of twenty-six boys and girls. I'd never felt
more alone in my life.

"As you see," Ms. Luskin announced, "Ian's

back with us. And I'm sure we're all glad to see him."

Everyone remained silent, leaning on their desks and looking at me the way they might stare at a magician who was performing a trick.

"Ian, why don't you take off that coat and stay awhile," Ms. Luskin said.

Didn't she know about my wings? The coat was my suit of armor, protecting me from the world. I couldn't take it off.

Then I felt Ms. Luskin's hands on the coat's shoulders. She slipped it over the tops of my wings and pulled it down until it tumbled to the floor.

There were gasps of surprise and astonishment. The students pointed at me and whispered among themselves. "Jeez!" I heard one boy murmur. "Now we've got another weirdo."

Ms. Luskin ignored the remark. But a few of the kids turned about to look at Anita Pickens, who sat in a far corner of the room. Anita wore ill-fitting homemade dresses and scuffed sandals, even in the winter. Her hair, long and straight, was tied up with a piece of leather shoestring. Until now, Anita had been considered the class freak.

She had six fingers on her left hand.

I was certain that I'd be replacing Anita as the room's oddball. My great wings made her extra finger seem as normal as sunrise.

I spotted Wayde Flack at his desk in the middle of the room. He kind of sneered back at me. "You should of said something before, Ian," he mumbled. "You should of told me about the wings when I called you on the phone."

"I couldn't—Mom and Dad wouldn't . . ."

"It's too late now," he said. Then he lowered his eyes. In an instant, without another word being spoken, the message was sent and received.

No more being friends, Ian. Your wings have changed all that. Just leave me alone.

Ms. Luskin clapped her hands for silence. "As you can see," she said, "Ian has grown wings." She didn't make a big deal of it. She might have been announcing that I'd had a haircut or that I was wearing a new pair of shoes. I stood up just a little straighter. She made the wings sound like an everyday kind of thing. I knew she was simply trying to ease my nervousness and embarrassment.

And I loved her for it.

"Now I know you're all curious about them," she went on. "So I wonder, Ian, if you'd spread them out so we can see how large and grand they really are."

With a jerk of my shoulders I spread the wings wide and flapped them slowly. The wind they created started blowing papers and chalk dust about the room.

"I think that's about enough of *that*," Ms. Luskin exclaimed. "Now that we've seen Ian's new wings, let's all get back to work. Ian, there's a stool and table over there. I'm sure you'll be comfortable."

She was wrong. It was hard to be at ease when all the kids were sneaking peeks at me and tittering behind their hands every time Ms. Luskin turned to write something on the blackboard.

After what seemed like a million years, the bell rang for lunch. Everybody got ready to go down to the cafeteria. I didn't want to leave the room and have a bunch of strangers seeing me the way I was.

"I have to go now," Ms. Luskin told me. "But I think you'd be better off staying here."

"I didn't bring any—"

"I'll have your lunch sent up. For now, I'll lock the door so nobody can come in unless you open it from inside."

The seventh graders filed out of the room, followed by Ms. Luskin. I heard her key turn in the lock. I was alone. I walked to the window and looked out over the playground. Soon, a few kids who'd wolfed their food down quickly in order to be first at the basketball courts and the baseball diamond came out below me, yelling and screaming and poking at one another in fake fights.

I wanted to be with them. I wanted to run and play and make jokes and do all the foolish wonderful things that only twelve-year-olds can dream up. I wanted to be normal.

There was a gentle knock on the classroom door. I moved along the wall so I wouldn't be seen and peeked quickly through the little window.

Anita Pickens was there, holding a cardboard tray on which was a cheese sandwich and a carton of milk. With her free hand—the one with six fingers—she motioned to me to open the door.

Reluctantly I turned the knob. Anita came in and handed me the tray. "Ms. Luskin told me to bring this to you," she said softly.

I took the tray. Anita turned to go. Then she paused.

"I . . . I'll stay, if you like."

I looked Anita up and down, from the thong-tied hair to the scuffed sandals. "Why?" I snapped bitterly. "So the two freaks can have a nice little talk, all by themselves?"

Without warning, Anita brought back her left arm and then snapped it forward. Her hand smacked against the side of my face with the sound of a whip cracking. The skin of her palm was rough and hard, and the muscles of her skinny arm had to have been made of steel cables. My vision was filled with red flashes, and my jaw felt as if it had been hit with a rock.

I stared at Anita, surprised. I'd never seen her get angry at anything before.

"Close your mouth," she said in that same soft, almost shy voice. "Are you trying to catch flies?"

"What . . . what did you do that for?" I gasped.

"I'm not used to being talked to that way when I'm doing a favor," she replied. "If you want to feel sorry for yourself on account of those wings, you go right ahead. But don't take it out on me."

"Hey, Anita, I'm—"

"Eat your lunch, Ian. I'm going outside."

For a few seconds my pride battled with my loneliness. Loneliness won.

"I—I'm sorry for what I said. I wish you'd stay."

"Why? So you can think up some more names to call me?"

"No. If I did it again, you might take my head clean off my shoulders. It's just . . . well, I haven't really talked to anybody for a long time."

"What about your parents—and your sister?"

"We argue a lot. And even then, they don't talk *to* me. They talk *at* me, if you know what I mean."

"Sure I know," Anita said. "Like you were something less than a real person because you're different. I get it all the time here in school."

"Yeah, but having an extra finger is nothing like growing—"

"You've only had those wings for a few weeks. I've been like this all my life."

Anita put her left hand flat against the blackboard. When she removed it, a moist print of its six fingers remained on the slate.

"The names are hard at first," she went on. "Like 'Spider-Hand.' If I remember right, you're the one who thought that one up. In fifth grade."

"I'm sorry, Anita."

"That's the second time you've been sorry in the last three minutes. I hope you don't plan on spending the rest of your life apologizing for things, just 'cause you've got those wings on your back."

"But I feel so . . . so different."

"Hey, you *are* different. So what? Who said everybody had to be just alike?"

"But nobody'll be friends with me anymore. Even Wayde Flack—"

"Then Wayde Flack can go jump in a bucket of hot tar. Anyhow, you've still got a friend."

"Oh? Who?"

"Me."

We sat silently for a long time. I ate my lunch, grateful for Anita's company. Finally the bell sounded to start the afternoon's classes.

"Those poor deprived kids who haven't got wings or extra fingers will be coming back in here," she said. "C'mon, Flyboy. Time to hit the books."

"Okay, Spider-Hand," I replied. We both laughed. It was the first time I'd laughed in a long time.

Somehow I got through the day. Every time I'd start feeling sorry for myself, I'd glance over at Anita. She seemed to know when I was looking, and she'd turn, smile, and wave her left hand. In spite of the six fingers, she moved it as gracefully as a tumbling leaf.

After school I waited in the classroom until

everybody else had had plenty of time to leave. Then I put on Dad's coat and scuttled through the halls to the door that led to the parking lot, where Dad had said he'd be waiting to drive me home.

He wasn't there.

The sun was high, and the day had gotten hot. Wearing Dad's coat, I felt like I was taking a steam bath. After a quick look around to see that nobody was watching, I shrugged off the coat and held it over my head to stand in its shade.

Just then, three ninth graders came around the corner of the building. One of them glanced at me, looked away, and then stared back with popping eyes.

"Wings," he said to his friends. "The kid's got wings."

"It's gotta be some kind of costume," said the tallest boy. The three walked toward me. "Hey, shorty, where'd you get the wings?"

They reached the place where I was standing, and the third boy—shorter than the others— pulled gently at one wing. "It's stuck on real good," he said. "Almost like it's growing there."

"It *is* growing there," I told him. I was really scared.

The tall boy grasped one wing tip, and the short one the other. They spread my wings wide. A bolt of pain shot up my back.

"Ow!" I cried. "Stop it!"

"He looks just like a big bat," said the third boy. "C'mon, kid. Fly for us."

"I . . . I can't fly. But my father's coming in a minute and—"

"Ah, go ahead. Try and fly. Pretend you're Peter Pan."

The two who held my wings started forcing them back and forth. I couldn't stand the pain. I began to cry.

"Look at us fly . . . up in the sky!" the tall boy chanted. "Hey, he's lighter'n he looks. We can almost lift him off the ground just by his wings."

My wings would be ripped off!

I tried to scream. A hand covered my mouth, and all I could manage was a muffled groan.

None of us saw the figure that came scurrying out of the building carrying a large metal garbage can. I heard a loud *clank* as the can was brought down on the short boy's head.

He fell onto the gravel, and Anita Pickens kicked him in the side, as hard as she could. The two other boys backed off. Anita, holding the can in front of her like a shield, stood beside me and faced them with her lips curled into a snarl.

"You take care of the one who's down, Ian," she told me. "If he makes a move, tear off his ears."

"It's three against two," said the tall boy. "Girl, I think we'd better teach you and Bat-Wings here a little lesson."

At that moment a battered pickup truck came roaring into the parking lot and screeched to a halt next to where we stood. The three boys paid it no attention. "Okay," the tall one said to Anita. "Now we're gonna—"

"You aren't gonna do anything!" called a voice from inside the truck. "Except get out of here. Right now!"

"Don't you tell me what . . ." Suddenly the boy's mouth flopped open, and his fists uncurled. He looked fearfully at his friends. Then all three dashed off around the corner of the building.

I turned to look at the side of the truck. The window, halfway down, caught the afternoon sun, and it was impossible to make out anything inside.

It wasn't hard, however, to see what had frightened off the ninth graders.

Poking through the opening above the glass was the barrel of a hunting rifle.

4

When the three boys had gone, the rifle barrel disappeared back into the truck and the side window slid down until it was completely open.

The face that appeared in the opening was like one of those carved wooden gnomes you can see in souvenir shops. It was weathered and tanned, with a small round nose that might have been a last-minute addition to the rest of the face. The head was covered by a large red scarf, tied under the chin.

"Hello, Mama," said Anita softly, as if fighting off three ninth graders was the most common thing in the world.

The truck door opened, and the woman got out. She was wearing a leather jacket, scratched and torn, over a dress of red and white checks that reached almost to her ankles.

"Who's this?" she asked, pointing at me.

"This is Ian, Mama. Ian Carras. Ian, this is my mama, Miz Maude Pickens."

"Hello, Ian," said Miz Pickens. "Anita doesn't have much in the way of friends. I'm pleased to meet you." As we shook hands, she saw my wings for the first time.

"What are those?" she asked Anita.

"Those're wings," said Anita simply.

"Some kind of costume, maybe?"

"Nope. They're real. Ian can flap 'em and everything."

Miz Pickens walked from side to side, inspecting me up and down. I felt her pluck at the wings with her knobby hand. I spread the wings wide and fanned them slowly back and forth.

"I never saw anything like that before in my life," said the woman.

"This is Ian's first day back at school since he grew 'em," Anita told her. "Those boys were pestering him, and I decided to take a hand."

"How many times have I told you, Anita, to act quiet and nice and stay out of fights? You could have hurt those lads real bad. Getting called names is no reason for you to get angry."

"But Mama, they were hurting Ian and pulling

on his wings, and I couldn't just stand by and watch."

"And what were you doing, hanging around after school?" Miz Pickens asked me.

"I was waiting for my father to pick me up, ma'am," I said. "He should have been here by now. But he's not."

"Then Ian, you just hop in the truck there. I'll have you home in a jiffy."

I looked inside the truck. There was only a single seat, covered with a faded blanket. The rifle Miz Pickens had used to scare away the boys now lay across a pair of deer horns mounted at the rear of the cab. A shift lever stuck up from the floor.

"I have to kneel on the seat because of my wings," I said. "If I get in, there won't be room enough for—"

"Then hop in the back," Miz Pickens said. "Just keep low, and don't spread those wings. It'll get pretty windy back there, once we start moving."

"Do I have to ride back there?" I bowed my head, and I could feel my face getting red. "Everybody will . . . I mean . . ."

"Ian's still getting used to having wings," Anita told her mother. "I don't think he's ready, just yet, for all the folks in town to see 'em."

"There's a piece of canvas on the truck bed. Lie down and throw it over you, and nobody'll know what my cargo is."

After telling Miz Pickens where I lived, I did as she said. It was dark under the canvas, and there was a thick smell of tarred cloth and pine sap. The doors slammed on both sides of the cab, the starter whirred, and the truck lurched forward with a loud clashing of gears.

After a short ride I felt the truck jolt to a stop. Both doors opened and were gently closed, not slammed. I was just about to throw off the canvas when a hand pressed me down against the bed of the truck.

"Stay still, boy," I heard Miz Pickens whisper. "Get real low when you pull that canvas off you. Then kind of peek over the side of the truck. You'll be able to see why your daddy couldn't come and pick you up at school."

I jerked away the canvas and raised myself until just my forehead and eyes cleared the truck's side. We were parked about fifty yards down the street from my house.

Our front yard was crammed with men and

women. Some seemed to be scribbling in note-books. Others had cameras and were taking pictures of everything in sight.

Our station wagon was standing in the drive-way. It was surrounded by a mob of people who were blocking it from backing into the street. Three television cameras were pointed at the wagon, and microphones were thrust toward its closed windows.

Whoever was in the car lowered the driver's side window. Through a brief opening in the crowd I saw my father's angry face. He shook his fist and shouted. The swarm of people gathered about, and the lens of a TV camera moved in until it was only a few inches from Dad's nose.

The window glided back up again.

"Reporters!" snapped Anita with a snort of disgust.

"Vultures is more like it," replied Miz Pickens as she looked down at me in the rear of the truck. "They got your daddy trapped there in the drive-way. And I'll bet I can guess what story they're looking for."

I nodded. "My wings."

"You may as well face it, Ian. There's no way

you can get home just now. If I was to turn you loose among that herd, they'd likely stomp you right into the ground, just to get something to write for their newspapers."

"But where will I go?"

"You let me and Anita worry about that. First, though, I've got to do something so your daddy can get back into his house."

"Can I help you, Mama?" asked Anita.

"Just hand me the gun from the rack there, if you please." Miz Pickens seemed as calm as if she were planning a trip to the grocery. "Now, Anita, you start the truck and get it ready to roll. We may want to leave in a hurry."

"But what about me?" I whispered.

"Keep low and out of sight," Miz Pickens ordered.

Peeking over the side of the truck, I saw Miz Pickens march toward the driveway with her rifle gripped in one gnarled hand. At the same time, Anita climbed into the front of the truck and started the engine.

Miz Pickens approached the crowd of newspaper and TV reporters surrounding the station wagon. She tried to speak to one or two of them, but nobody paid any attention. They were too interested in shouting questions through the windows at my father.

Miz Pickens backed off a short distance from the crowd. She pointed the rifle at the ground.

BAM

All at once the shouting and murmuring turned into an eerie silence. Everybody looked at Miz Pickens as she shucked the empty shell from her rifle and rammed a new one into place. Then there was a loud yell from one of the TV cameramen.

"Jeez, lady! You could have shot my foot off!"

From that distance I couldn't hear Miz Pickens' answer. But whatever it was, it sure made that guy mad!

First he shook his fist. Then he lifted the huge camera off his shoulder and laid it on the ground. He took a single step toward Miz Pickens.

She moved the rifle slightly.

BAM

The man froze. He looked from Miz Pickens to the camera on the ground and back again. Then he howled in outrage.

"You . . . you shot my camera!"

Miz Pickens merely nodded.

"D'you know how much one of those things costs? I could—"

"You could all go home and leave this man in peace!" shouted Miz Pickens. She worked the bolt of the rifle again. "Now I've already wasted two shots! No telling where the third might go. So GIT!"

They got. Slowly at first, and then faster, they moved away from the station wagon, looking for hiding places.

I saw Dad and Miz Pickens having a hurried, whispered conversation. Then Dad drove the wagon into the garage. Behind him the big door hummed closed.

Miz Pickens scuttled back to the truck. As Anita revved the engine, her mother climbed in the passenger side.

"Quick now, Anita. Drive us away from here before one of those reporters takes it in his head to come following. Ian, you get down beneath that canvas again. They aren't sure where you're at. I intend to keep it that way."

She slammed the door. Anita spun the truck into a U-turn and raced off down the street while Miz Pickens placed the rifle back on the deer-horn rack. I pulled the canvas over my head and held it tightly.

For several minutes the ride was smooth. Then the truck veered hard right, and I was tossed about as the tires wobbled over rocks and into ruts. We seemed to be on a steep hill, and I heard Anita downshift a couple of times, while the old motor roared in protest and the metal truck bed bumped and vibrated against my stomach.

I was dumbfounded by what I was discovering about Anita Pickens. I'd always thought of her as just a shy girl who had little to say in school and kept to herself most of the time. She'd always taken the teasing about her extra finger in silence, without ever getting mad. Oh, she did well enough in her schoolwork. But while the rest of us in the class were running, shouting, and fooling around on the playground equipment, she usually would be sitting off somewhere, reading or simply staring at the mountains around our village.

A real nerd, I'd always thought.

But today she'd slapped my face—hard—when I'd insulted her. Then she'd fought those ninth graders when I'd been too scared to do anything. She'd waited calmly while Miz Pickens was with the reporters, as if shooting a TV camera were the most common thing in the world. Now she was handling the truck with the skill of a race-car driver.

Anita had been in my class since third grade. And I suddenly discovered I didn't really know her at all.

The truck careened around a final corner, bumped across what felt like a plowed field, and lurched to a stop. I heard the doors open, and then Miz Pickens was pulling the canvas away from my face. I squinted my eyes against the afternoon sun.

"Come on out of there, Ian," Miz Pickens said. "You're safe now."

I unwrapped myself and sat up. We were parked in the middle of a large, flat field. Around me, several huge boulders poked up through the earth. The mountains didn't seem as high as they had down in the village. I soon discovered why.

We were nearly at the top of one of them.

Anita and Miz Pickens had plowed a garden into the rocky earth. A thick forest of pines and hardwood trees surrounded the clearing. Near the middle was the cabin.

It was made of rough-cut boards that had never

known a coat of paint. On each side there was a single window, and a black stovepipe stuck out of the cedar-shingled roof. A small porch guarded the front—and only—door. It was not a city house. But off here in the mountains it seemed to fit right in.

"We're home, Ian," said Miz Pickens as she unlatched the rear of the truck and helped me down. For a second I thought I was going to fall, but by flapping my wings I got my balance.

"Home?" I said. "But my home's back in town."

"Get real, Ian," said Anita. "We couldn't leave you off with all those reporters ready to grab at you. They'd have been worse than those boys at school."

"I told your pa where you'd be," added Miz Pickens. "He'll get in touch, soon as he can."

"But won't the reporters come up here?"

"I expect so. But it may take 'em a while to find out where you are. We're just fine for the time being."

I wasn't at all sure I wanted to be off in the mountains with these two strange people. I felt tears fill my eyes and start rolling down my cheeks.

"Now don't start blubbering, Ian," said Miz Pickens with an impatient wave of her hand. "Your troubles won't last forever. Before you know it, your pa will be calling you on the phone."

She pointed to wires that came out of the clearing and stretched to the house. The poles that held up the wires were the dead but still rooted trunks of trees.

"My late husband, Leland, was a logger for the Faraday Lumber Company, which owns a lot of the land hereabouts," said Miz Pickens. "One day not long after Anita was born, he was out in the forest, felling a tree. Only this time the tree twisted on its stump and fell the wrong way. Poor Leland had no time to get out of the way."

A look of sadness passed over her face. Then it was replaced with a faint smile.

"The Faraday Company took real good care of Anita and me. I was hired to look after things in this part of their woods, and they put up this house for us to live in. We have most of the comforts. There's a telephone and electricity and about everything else—except inside water. If you want running water, you've got to run for it. There's a spring over by that flat rock. It freezes in winter, but then there's snow for melting."

"Winter?" I gasped.

"Oh, we're not going to keep you here that long. A few days, at most."

"But what about school?"

"Just for now, you won't be going to school, Ian. That's the first place those reporters will go looking."

"But everybody knows about my wings already. So what—"

"The reporters still want to get at *you*, Ian," said Anita. "They'd be snapping your picture and pestering you with questions and grabbing at your wings all hours of the day and night. Me and Ma are going to see that doesn't happen to you. As for school, I'll bring your lessons home every day. We can study together. I'll see you keep right up with the rest of the class."

We walked into the cabin. Its main area was a kitchen and living room, all in one. There was an old electric stove and a refrigerator in one corner, and next to them a sink with a drainpipe but no faucets. A pair of stools stood underneath the metal-topped table. Rough shelves and cupboards were on all four walls, and on the braided rug that covered much of the floor were an overstuffed chair with a patch on one arm and a rocker. An opening was cut out of the ceiling, and a ladder led up to it.

"You'll sleep in there," said Miz Pickens, pointing to a door in one wall. "Usually it's my room, but for now I'll bed down in the loft with Anita. When you have to heed the call of nature, the necessary's the little shack out in back. When you use it, be sure and close the door so we'll know it's occupied."

She took a deep breath. "That's about it, Ian—so welcome. After all the excitement, I expect you could use something to eat."

With that, Miz Pickens walked into the "kitchen" and began rummaging through the refrigerator. I gazed forlornly about.

Then I felt Anita place her hand gently in mine. Her six fingers wrapped about my palm and squeezed gently. "It'll be fine, Ian," she said softly. "You'll see."

My great wings spread out behind me, brushing against the wall as they fanned the air. "Anita, I . . . I . . ."

"Sit down and rest. Would you like the easy chair or the rocker?"

"I can't . . . my wings . . ."

She brought one of the stools and I slumped down onto it. My wings folded onto their resting position against my back.

"D'you want to talk about . . . about anything?" Anita asked.

"No, I—"

"Then we'll just sit here and be quiet." Gripping my hand again, she sank into the easy chair.

We stayed there, almost without moving, until supper was ready.

Later, after we'd eaten, I said I'd like to call home. "The telephone's right there," said Anita.

I dialed our number, and Dad answered on the second ring. "I told you people to stop calling here!" he yelled, loud enough to set my ear ringing. "And if you—"

"Dad, it's me—Ian."

"Oh."

Then I heard Mom on the extension. "Are . . . are you all right, Son?"

"Yeah, Mom. I'm okay. We had tomato soup and cheese sandwiches for supper. And Miz—"

"No names, Son!" said Dad quickly. "You never can tell who's listening in. Chances are those reporters are connected into our telephone line."

"I miss . . . I miss . . ." My eyes grew warm, and tears blurred my vision.

"It's better this way," Dad told me. "There's no real story until they locate you. In the meantime, my committee can prepare a statement about . . ."

I gripped the receiver hard. I wanted to crush it. I was alone and scared, and all Dad could talk about was how he could become mayor. My wings folded and unfolded as I felt anger churning inside me.

"Mom!" I shouted. "Let me talk to Mom!"

"I'm here, Ian," she replied.

"Mom, I can't stand this. Can't we all just leave Blanton and move away somewhere and . . . and . . ."

"You're being silly," she told me. "Your father can't just give up his work at the bank and the election and all. And the doctor thinks he may have found someone to do the . . . well, you know. In just a little while everything will be back to normal. You'll see."

Normal? How could anything be normal while the wings sprouted from my shoulders?

In the receiver I heard a sudden gasp, and then Dad was yelling. "You with the red shirt—get away from that window!"

"The reporters are still outside," Mom told me.

"I've got to phone the police," Dad cried out. "Good-bye, Ian. We'll be in touch."

There was a click as the connection was broken.

I turned about. Anita was back in the easy chair. There was a concerned look on her face, and she was shaking her head slowly from side to side.

"They couldn't talk much," I said. "The reporters . . ."

Suddenly I sank to my knees and buried my face in my hands. My body shook. The sound of flapping wings was loud inside the cabin.

5

That night, lying in Miz Pickens's narrow bed, I had trouble sleeping. For one thing, I was embarrassed. When I'd had to go outside to the one-hole "necessary" shack, my wings had made it impossible for me to fit inside. I had to walk into the woods. Miz Pickens and Anita hadn't said anything when I'd returned to the cabin, but from the looks on their faces, I saw they knew about my problem.

Besides that, I missed my own house and my own room and my parents and even Diane. I couldn't help wondering how long I'd be stuck off in a mountain cabin, with only Miz Pickens and Anita for company.

The next morning I woke up late. I had a lot of trouble putting on my clothes. The Velcro fastenings were hard to close without help. Finally I finished and walked out into the cabin's main room.

Nobody was there. For a moment I started to panic. Then I saw the penciled note on the table.

Ian—

I am taking Anita to school, and then I have to buy some supplies. Back in a while. Make yourself at home. There is cereal in the cupboard and milk in the ice box. Get your own breakfast. The tub by the sink needs to be filled with water from the spring. You'll find a bucket on the porch.

So I was not to be a pampered guest, but more like a working member of the family. I liked that. I poured cereal into a bowl and slopped milk over it. Usually I have sugar on my cereal, but I couldn't find it so I did without.

Afterward I filled the tub. It took sixteen trips to the spring and back. Miz Pickens still hadn't returned, so I decided to look around and see what my new home was like.

I walked around the edge of the clearing. Forests covered three sides of it. When I got to the fourth, I found myself at the top of a sheer rock wall at least two hundred feet high. I got down on my stomach and peered over the edge. Far below I could see the tops of trees. The forest stretched off into the distance, covering the mountains like a great green blanket.

"This is no place for somebody who walks in their sleep, Ian. If you was to fall off there, they'd be hard put even to find your dead body down below."

I turned my head. Miz Pickens had returned and was standing above me. "Beautiful view, though," she went on. "Here, let me help you up."

Reaching around my folded wings, she put her hands under my armpits and lifted. I popped to my feet like a jack-in-the-box.

"Land sakes, Ian!" Miz Pickens exclaimed. "You don't weigh much more'n a handful of wood shavings. I'll have to feed you up while you're here. Still, you don't appear scrawny. It is a wonder."

We walked back to the truck, and I helped her carry groceries inside and put them away. Then I just stood there, waiting for something else to do.

"What are you hanging about for, Ian?" Miz Pickens demanded finally.

"Do you have some other jobs for me?" I asked.

"Not just now. Once Anita gets home with your work, school starts for you. But for the present why don't you just go out and play?"

I went outside. I had no playmates and nothing to play with. I just stood there, wondering how to amuse myself.

Except for exercise in the cellar, I wasn't allowed to flap my wings at home. But here on the mountain there was almost endless space. I spread the wings wide and flapped them loudly, watching the clumps of grass bend in the wind I created.

Next I tried climbing one of the huge boulders that stuck out of the ground. Halfway up, the slick soles of my school shoes began to slide, and I almost toppled backward. Instinctively I moved my wings and righted myself, hopping back to the ground like a crow coming down off a fence post.

Hey, that was fun! I climbed back onto the rock and scrabbled all the way to the top. Then, as I leaped off into space, I flapped my wings furiously. Slowly I drifted downward until my feet touched the earth as lightly as feathers.

I tried it again . . . and again. This was more fun than jumping from our garage roof using an umbrella as a parachute.

My shoulders began to ache. I folded the wings against my back and looked about. High in the sky a hawk hung motionless, looking for prey below.

Like me, the hawk had wings. But it could fly.

Suddenly I wondered if I . . .

After a short rest, I went to the center of the clearing. I spread my wings wide and moved them gently in the still air.

Then, when I was really ready, I began pumping the wings up and down, up and down, as hard as I could. *FLAP . . . FLAP . . .* The sound was loud in my ears. I could feel sweat break out on my face from the effort, and great clouds of dust billowed up from the dry soil. Slowly I rose up onto my tiptoes.

But that was as far as I could go. I could not break free from the pull of gravity. My back seemed to be on fire from the pain of my effort.

I rested. Somewhere I'd read about dodos and ostriches and other birds of ancient and modern times that had wings but were not able to fly.

That was me—just another dodo.

I walked to the spring and splashed water on my face to wash away the dust. When I turned back to the cabin, I saw Miz Pickens, standing at a window and looking out at me. I wondered how long she'd been watching.

That afternoon Miz Pickens said she had a job

for me. From under the porch she pulled out a saw
nearly four feet long, with huge teeth on its lower
edge. "Ever cut wood before, Ian?" she asked me.

"No, ma'am. But I'm willing to learn."

She led me to a pile of dead tree trunks near the
garden patch. "Saw 'em about this long," she said,
slicing the butt from one log with a dozen strokes
of the saw. "Any longer and they won't fit in the
stove next winter."

She handed me the saw. I set it on top of a trunk
and began jerking it back and forth with my right
arm.

"You'll get nowhere that way," said Miz Pickens. "It's all done with the back. Your arm is just
along for the ride. Like this."

She demonstrated, and the saw slid through the
wood easily.

I caught the rhythm and was soon hard at work.
Miz Pickens nodded approvingly. "I'm off to pick
up Anita at school," she said. "I won't be gone
long."

The day was cool and the saw sharp. I worked
on without stopping. I delighted in the harsh rasp-
ing of the saw, the tumbling of each piece of wood
as I cut it away, and the rapidly shrinking pile of

tree trunks. I imagined the wood being split and then poked into the pot-bellied stove to make the cabin warm through the long winter.

"Mama just asked you to cut some wood, Ian. You don't have to kill yourself."

I looked around. Miz Pickens and Anita were standing behind me.

"From the looks of that pile of cut wood, you've been working pretty steady," said Miz Pickens. "Don't you need a rest?"

"No. I'm fine, really. I don't know when I've felt better."

Suddenly I heard a tearing sound as Anita parted the Velcro strips on my shirt. I felt it being lifted above my wings.

"Would you look at that!" I heard Miz Pickens exclaim.

"What? What is it? Is something wrong?"

"Not really wrong," replied Anita. Her hand slipped beneath my folded wings and moved along my skin. "The muscles here look and feel like you've been working out with weights or something. All bulging and thick, like knots in a rope. I never saw anything like it, except in the strength magazines at the drugstore. Have you been doing a lot of exercising to get this way?"

Only my attempts at flying earlier that day, I said to myself. But a few minutes of that wouldn't explain the kind of thing Anita had described. I shook my head.

"It does beat all," said Miz Pickens. "But you'd better stop now and get to your schoolwork. Anita's brought your books, and she'll give you all the help you need."

As I headed toward the cabin, Anita and Miz Pickens put their heads together and began whispering to one another excitedly. Anita nodded a couple of times, and Miz Pickens had a big smile on her face.

Anita gave me two hours of "lessons" before dinner. First she opened the literature book. "The story we read today was real special," she told me. "Ms. Luskin said she was sorry you weren't there, for she picked it out especially for you. Course, I never told her about you staying up here."

The tale was of Daedalus and Icarus. Although it was an ancient myth, I could imagine myself in every word of it. Daedalus had made wings for himself and his son, and they'd actually flown with them. When I finished, I turned to Anita.

"I tried to fly today," I told her. "It didn't work."

Anita looked beyond me at Miz Pickens, who was preparing dinner. I turned about on my stool just in time to see Miz Pickens wink broadly at her daughter. They seemed to be sharing some secret that I wasn't in on.

Later, Anita tried to explain the mysteries of photosynthesis. "The sun comes shining down on the leaves of a plant," she said. "And when that happens, the plant makes food. Just from the sunlight and what it gets from the earth. That's really something, isn't it, Ian?"

I couldn't concentrate on science. I was too fascinated by the way Anita moved her hands to illustrate the lesson. The six fingers of her left hand became beams of sunlight, shining downward and finally touching the leaf that was her other palm.

The hands fluttered gracefully through the air like a pair of butterflies, and her large brown eyes followed them intently.

"Spider-Hand" I'd called her. But she wasn't a freak.

She was beautiful.

Behind me I heard a loud sizzling as Miz Pickens slammed a big piece of meat into a hot skillet.

"I'd like my steak rare!" I announced. Then, more softly: "If . . . if you don't mind, Miz Pickens."

"Mama has to cook it clear through," said Anita. "If bear meat isn't cooked well, it can sicken you when you eat it."

"Bear meat?" I asked with a gulp.

"That's right. Last winter that animal almost tore the porch right off this place, trying to get inside. Mama shot it and froze the best parts for when we have special company. That's you, Ian."

My stomach churned at the very idea of eating such stuff. "I've never— That is, I guess I don't want any bear meat."

"Then a helping of carrots is all you're getting," replied Miz Pickens sharply. "I dunno how your folks ran things. But here you'll eat what's put in front of you, or you go hungry."

I ate the meat. It was delicious.

About nine o'clock that evening, we were sitting around the kitchen table playing dominos when I saw Anita glance out the window. "A car's coming," she announced. "I can see the lights. D'you suppose it's one of those reporters?"

"If it is," replied Miz Pickens, "he won't be here long." She got up, reached into the rear of a closet, and pulled out an ancient double-barreled shotgun. Then she went out on the porch just as the car made its final turn and stopped at the edge of the clearing.

"You in the car!" she bawled. "You see what I've got in my hand. Now state your business."

"It's just me, Miz Pickens."

"Don't shoot!" I cried, running out onto the porch. "It's Dad!"

"He'd better learn to call on the telephone when he's coming up here," Miz Pickens told me. "I like to know ahead of time who's paying a visit."

"Maybe he's coming to take me back home," I said hopefully.

There was a sound of footsteps, and then my father came out of the darkness and into the circle of light from the open front door. He was carrying a large suitcase.

"This is for you, Ian." He handed me the case. "Extra clothes."

So I'd be staying at the cabin at least awhile longer.

Miz Pickens ushered us all inside. She sat in the

rocker, and Dad took the easy chair. Anita and I dragged out stools from under the kitchen table.

"It's a good thing you brought extra clothes for Ian," said Miz Pickens. "Around here, doing the laundry is a sometimes thing."

"I thought that with Ian out of the way, those reporters would leave," my father said. "But they're still chasing all over the place, trying to find him. I got a court order to keep them off my property, but there they stand, with their toes right on the boundary line. I had to slip out after dark and borrow a neighbor's car just to get up here without being followed."

Dad leaned back against the chair's cushions and took a deep breath. "Miz Pickens," he went on, "for the present, your cabin is about the only place on earth where my son's . . . uh . . . deformity can be kept out of the public eye."

"Ian's welcome to stay until those reporters leave, if that's what you were about to ask."

My father nodded. "You see, I'm running for mayor, and . . . well, the voters just wouldn't understand."

"I'm doing it for the boy's sake—not for yours."

Dad looked as if she'd suddenly slapped him.

"I . . . I'd be happy to make it worth your while," he mumbled.

"Money? Don't cheapen your own son any further with talk of money."

"And what's *that* supposed to mean?" asked Dad in an angry voice.

"Because of his wings, Ian's in an impossible situation with all those reporters hanging about. Seems to me that you ought to be worrying about how he feels. But all I've heard so far is that you're worried about getting enough votes to be mayor."

"It's just more convenient now to . . . to have Ian out of the way. As for the money, I'm sure you'll have expenses and—"

"Ian'll pull his own weight. I'll see to that. He's a good worker, Mr. Carras. Both my daughter and I would enjoy having him stay here awhile."

"That's just great," said Dad with a sigh of relief. "And either Mrs. Carras or I will call as often as we can to—"

"Once a day will be plenty," Miz Pickens said. "If he's to be here, he'll abide by my rules, and I'll see to his welfare. I'll not have you and your wife looking over my shoulder all the time and telling me what to do."

"But we're his parents!"

"Uh-huh. And those wings he's grown horrify you. Don't try to deny it, for it's written all over your face. I'd imagine Ian's mother feels the same way. But the wings don't horrify me, no more than the sixth finger on my daughter's hand does. They're facts of life, and I've learned to accept such facts and move on from there."

"Hey now! I don't have to sit and listen to—"

"Yes you do . . . if you want Ian staying here. Yesterday I brought up to this cabin a poor wretched boy who'd been beaten down by every human contact. Even his own family was ashamed of him.

"This afternoon, Mr. Carras, Ian cut up a whole pile of wood for me. And d'you know what he said when he was done? 'I don't know when I've felt better,' that's what. Did you ever think you'd hear Ian say something like that?"

"Well, I . . . I . . ."

I'd never before seen my father at a loss for words. For the first time I began to think that having wings wasn't quite as bad as I'd supposed.

"I've reached the end of my lecture, Mr. Carras," growled Miz Pickens. "So if you've got no more to say, you can go to—"

"There is something else," said Dad. "If Ian's to stay here, you should be aware of it."

"Of what?" asked Miz Pickens.

"Ian's weight loss. According to Dr. Donovan, it's primarily in the skeleton—the bones."

"Are you saying Ian's got some disease that—"

"No. Not exactly. As I understand it, his bones are no longer heavy and solid, like those of other humans. They've grown hollow and light—like the skeleton of a bird."

"I see." Miz Pickens turned to Anita and winked one eye—just as she'd done earlier, during my lesson. I wondered what secret they were sharing.

"And now, sir," said Miz Pickens, turning back to my father, "if you've nothing else to tell me, I'd suggest you get back to town before those reporters get wind of where you are."

I said good-bye to my father and then went into my room. In spite of being awake most of last night and all the work I'd done, I wasn't tired.

I was terrified.

I could practically feel my bones getting lighter and lighter.

Would they soon disappear altogether? I wondered. I imagined myself as I might appear—a mound of flesh like a gigantic sponge, with no skeleton at all.

A sponge with wings.

Sleep was a long time coming.

6

The next day, the helicopter appeared.

Miz Pickens brought Anita home from school and then announced that she'd be taking her monthly report to the logging-company office. "Mr. Hawes, the boss man, always takes me to a restaurant for dinner when I bring in my report," she told me. "So you two will have to shift for yourselves to get something to eat."

"Ian and I will be just fine, Mama," Anita said. "You just go and have a good time."

With that, Miz Pickens got in the truck and roared back down the hill. Anita and I began our schoolwork.

Anita heard it first. She was showing me how to divide one fraction by another when suddenly she put a finger to her lips. "Listen, Ian," she said softly.

I listened. There was a faint sound, like someone

tapping a rolled newspaper with a ruler. It seemed to be coming closer.

Anita went to the door and opened it. She shaded her eyes and looked upward. The sound got louder and louder.

"It's a helicopter," Anita said. "Looks like it's getting ready to set down out by our garden."

"Maybe it's having engine trouble," I said.

"Maybe. But I doubt it. I'll bet somebody's discovered you're up here, and they're looking for you."

I started to get scared. My wings beat wildly, and the school papers on the kitchen table were blown away by the breeze I created. "Shouldn't we run?" I asked in a quavering voice.

"They'd see us for sure, soon as we set foot outside," said Anita.

"Then what . . ."

"Now don't you worry, Ian. I believe I can handle this, even without Mama's help."

By now the *whap-whap-whap* of the rotor blades was almost deafening. Anita opened the door of the closet where the shotgun was kept. She fumbled around among the coats and dresses in there and dragged it out. To me the weapon looked as huge as a cannon.

"Anita, you're not thinking about—" I began.

"Maybe whoever's in that helicopter should have something to think about," she replied. She opened the shotgun, peered inside, and smiled to herself.

There was one last roar from the helicopter's engine, a final whirring of rotor blades, and then silence. "You go into your room and stay out of sight," Anita ordered.

"But you can't—"

"I'll handle this. Don't you worry about a thing."

I wanted to stay and see how Anita "handled" the situation. But I wasn't going to argue. I walked into my room. However, I couldn't resist keeping the door open a crack so I could see as well as hear what went on.

A rapping at the door. Anita opened it.

In the doorway stood a man in a brown suit. A camera hung from a strap around his neck. Behind him was another man, in the uniform of a state policeman.

"Mrs. Pickens?" asked the man with the camera. "Mrs. Maude Pickens?"

"She's not available." Anita cradled the shotgun almost lovingly in her arms. "State your business, mister."

"I'm Stanley Bartok of the Silver City *Sentinel*," the man replied. "And this policeman is—"

"Officer Munson has been a friend to Mama and me for a long time," said Anita. "How's the family, Mr. Munson?"

"Just fine, Anita," said the officer.

"And why did you come up here with this reporter fella?"

"Mr. Bartok just wanted me along to make sure—"

"Miss Pickens, I—" Bartok began.

"I would be obliged, Mr. Bartok, if you wouldn't crowd the doorway. You can do all your talking right there on the porch."

Bartok, who had been inching forward, froze in his tracks. His eyes never left the shotgun in Anita's hands. "None of the other reporters down in the village have any idea where Ian Carras is," he said. "But I saw the license on your truck when you left the Carras place, and I found out where you live. I want an exclusive story for my paper. So if I could just talk to the boy and maybe get a picture or two—"

"I am sorry, Mr. Bartok. I guess you came a long way for nothing. If . . . *if* there's somebody staying

here with Mama and me, that person's got the
right not to be disturbed by some nosy reporter.
Can you understand that?"

Anita's bravery astonished me. I'd never have
dared to stand up to Bartok the way she was doing
it.

"The people have a right to know—" sputtered
Bartok.

"A twelve-gauge shotgun is an interesting
weapon," said Anita calmly, as if she were discuss-
ing the weather. "Especially one loaded with double-aught shot." She fondled the gun lovingly.

"Are you trying to intimidate—"

"Mama told me once about a hunting accident.
A fella took a load of double-aught, full in the
belly. Oh, the hole where it went in wasn't much.
Only about as big around as his thumb. But
around in back, where the shot came out? A real
mess, Mama said. Of course the man himself
didn't care. He was dead."

I saw Bartok lurch backward. Both his face and
Munson's were pasty white.

"Did . . . did you hear her threaten me?" Bartok
sputtered. "Officer Munson, I demand that you
disarm this girl."

The policeman didn't move. He just kept staring at the shotgun.

"Oh, I wasn't threatening," said Anita innocently. "I was just talking about something my mama told me."

"I wonder, Miss Pickens," said Bartok, "if you have any idea of the trouble you're causing with your stubbornness. My editor is a close personal friend of the governor. And he—"

"My, my," said Anita. "The governor. What do you think of that, Mr. Munson?"

Munson licked his lips nervously. "I do wish you'd put down that gun, Anita," he whispered. "Something like that in the hands of a little girl like you . . . well, there might be an awful accident."

Anita shook her head. "Mama taught me all about handling guns. This one won't shoot unless I want it to."

"But the governor!" Munson said in a quavering voice. "He's kind of—kind of my boss, Anita. His word is law!"

"That's right, Anita," said Bartok, a little more bravely. "So if you'll just step aside . . ."

Anita jabbed the gun at Bartok's belly. "Mr.

Bartok, if you take one more step, I'll pull both these triggers at once."

"But didn't you hear what Munson just said? Now stop being foolish and—"

"Mr. Munson, you talked about the law just now. Well, my teacher, Ms. Luskin, told me something about law, just the other day. And Ms. Luskin's not in the habit of lying."

"What did your teacher say?" Munson asked.

"We've been studying the Bill of Rights of the U.S. Constitution. I remember Article Four really well. It says nobody can come searching in a person's house unless they've got reason to believe there's been a crime. Even then, they have to bring a paper from a judge, saying the search is legal."

"But—"

"Of course, maybe I didn't really understand what Ms. Luskin was saying. So I'll leave it up to you, Mr. Munson. Is that the law of the land or not?"

The policeman nodded. "The words in the Constitution are fancier. But you've got the gist of it, Anita."

He turned to Bartok. "I don't think the governor would want to get mixed up in this one. Why, if word got out, he'd lose the next election by a land-slide."

"I'm going to make a phone call now," said Anita, backing away from the door. "You just stay out there on the porch, Mr. Bartok. One move to come inside, and I pull both triggers. Mr. Munson, if this gun was to go off, you might get hurt, too. But Mama says you can't make an omelette with-out breaking some eggs."

Still gripping the shotgun, Anita lifted the tele-phone receiver with her free hand. Setting the re-ceiver down, she dialed a number and then put the receiver to her ear.

"Mr. Hawes?" she said. "Anita Pickens here. I'm so glad you and Mama are still there. May I speak to her, please?"

There was a short pause. Then Anita began tell-ing everything that had happened since we had first heard the helicopter.

Another pause.

"I see, Mama. . . . Can Mr. Hawes do that, right quick? Oh, that would be just fine. 'Bye, Mama. And do tell Mr. Hawes how obliged we are for the help."

She hung up the receiver and returned to the doorway.

"Seems like you've got no right being here, Mr. Bartok," she told the reporter. "Mama's having Mr. Hawes from the lumber company get something called a restraining order from a judge. The way I understand it, none of you newspaper people will be allowed to come up here or even fly over in an airplane or a helicopter."

"You little—"

"Faraday Lumber owns a lot of land around here," Anita went on. "So I don't think Mr. Hawes will have any trouble getting that order. Nor making it stick, either."

"But this is the story of the year. Think of my readers!"

"You think of 'em. Me, I'm Ian's friend. Mama and I are about the only friends he's got just now. We don't understand why he should be plagued by you reporters, just so a lot of nosy folks can have something to chuckle over while they're drinking their morning coffee."

Suddenly Bartok spun about and stepped down off the porch. "Come on, Munson!" he snapped. "Let's get out of here."

They strode off toward the helicopter. There was a high whine as the pilot, who'd been waiting inside the plastic bubble, started the engine.

I came out of the bedroom and watched as the machine took off, raising a cloud of dust around the cabin.

"Anita," I sputtered, "I want to . . . I mean . . . well . . ."

"If you're trying to say thanks, then you're welcome," she replied.

"But would you really have shot them?"

Anita stepped out onto the porch. She put the gun to her shoulder and aimed at the helicopter, high overhead. Her fingers yanked both triggers at the same time.

CLICK

I blinked in surprise. "Did you know that gun wasn't loaded?" I asked.

"Sure did," she replied with a grin. "If I was to greet anybody—no matter who—with a loaded shotgun, Mama'd paddle me until she raised blisters. Still, Mama doesn't hold with telling fibs, so I took care never to actually lie to those two and say the gun was loaded. What they chose to believe was their business."

After the lessons, we had a meal of cold cuts and potato salad. "I'm surprised your mother isn't back by now," I told Anita.

"Why? Mama wouldn't miss her monthly dinner with Mr. Hawes for anything. She knows I can take care of things here while she's away."

"But you were in trouble, and—"

"Trouble? Not from Bartok and Mr. Munson. As long as I was holding the shotgun, those two would listen to reason. Now the bear who tried to bust in here last winter was real trouble. We couldn't talk it into leaving, so Mama finally had to shoot it."

Anita and I were washing the dishes when Dad called.

"That gang of news hounds outside won't budge," he told me bitterly. "Even without you here, they manage to find something to write. At this rate, I'll have about as much chance of being elected mayor as . . ."

He went on and on about politics and how he was sure he was losing votes and how bad he was feeling about the whole thing until I couldn't stand it anymore.

"You . . . you make me sick!" I howled into the mouthpiece.

I wanted to tear the phone out of the wall and hurl it through a window. Couldn't dad think about anything except himself?

"Don't you talk to me that way, Ian Carras. I'm your father!"

"And I'm your son. But sometimes I wish I wasn't!"

"I've heard enough. Here, Madeline. See if you can talk some sense into him."

The next voice on the phone was Mom's. "Hello, Ian dear. Are you getting along all right up there?"

"Yeah, Mom. Just fine."

"Then why do you have to get your father so upset? He's under a great strain just now, you know."

"Yeah?" I replied sarcastically. "But what about me?"

"You, Ian?"

"Yeah, me, Me, *ME*. I'm the one with these damn wings growing out of my back!"

"Ian, I don't want to listen to such disgusting language."

"Okay, then listen to this!" I held the receiver at arm's length. At the same time I flapped my wings, beating the air with loud fluttering sounds.

"What . . . what's that noise?"

"My wings, Mom. The wings you and Dad hate

so much. Well, I hate them, too. And I hate . . . I hate . . ."

I hated my parents. But I couldn't bring myself to say it.

I smashed the receiver back onto its hook. Then I put my face against the wall and sobbed, feeling guilty and ashamed.

I felt Anita's hands on my shoulders. She didn't say a word. What was there to say?

When I finally stopped bawling, she handed me a damp towel to wash my face. While I was doing that, I heard her turn on the radio and dial it to a station that was playing slow music.

As I tossed the towel into the sink, she held out both hands.

"Come, Ian."

"But what . . . ?"

"That music's real pretty. Come and dance with me."

"I don't know much about dancing."

"Me neither. A girl with a spider hand don't get too many chances at it. But maybe we can teach each other."

I went to her. We danced—if you could call it that. I held her as if she might break and plodded

about with the grace of a trained bear. It was a
risky business for Anita. I stepped on her toes a
few times, and she kept tangling her fingers in my
wings.

But while I was concentrating on getting those
steps right, I almost forgot my feelings about Mom
and Dad.

Finally the band on the radio gave way to a talk
show. We let our arms drop to our sides.

"Thank you, Ian," Anita said solemnly, as if we
were in an elegant ballroom instead of a crude
cabin. "You were wonderful."

Wonderful? How wonderful could it have been,
getting her toes crushed and having a partner who
was shaking from nervousness and at the same
time stiff as a board?

I guessed I'd never understand how girls' minds
worked.

When Miz Pickens got home later that evening,
Anita and I filled her in on all the details of Bartok's visit. When we were done, she laughed loud
and long.

"I don't guess those critters'll be back real soon,"
she said. "Mr. Hawes phoned the judge, and even

if Bartok tells the rest where you are, they won't be allowed near here. But before we turn in to bed, I need to hear the weather report."

At that, she winked at Anita, just as she'd done the day before. Anita smiled back.

These two have some secret, I thought. And they weren't sharing it with me. "Are you always this interested in the weather?" I asked Miz Pickens.

"Nope. But they say that Saturday's going to be bright and sunny—just perfect for a little party Anita and I are planning."

"A party? You mean with a lot of people and—"

"Nope. Just you, me, and Anita. And you, Ian, are going to be the guest of honor!"

7

Saturday dawned bright and clear. I was the first one up, all excited by the idea of a party—with me as the guest of honor.

But what kind of a party would it be with just the three of us? We saw each other every day, so there wasn't anything new to talk about. Maybe there'd be a cake and lemonade, but after we'd had that, things might get kind of boring.

No. Anita and Miz Pickens were many things, but they were never boring. There'd be something going on. Maybe we'd go exploring in the woods and find . . . oh . . . an abandoned mine or something like that. Or maybe . . . I just didn't know. It was a mystery, and I couldn't wait to find the answer.

I got dressed, came out into the main room, and peered through the east window. The great red ball of sun was perched on top of the mountains like

a gigantic cherry on a huge dish of green ice cream.
I opened the refrigerator and began rummaging
among its contents. If Anita and her mother slept
a little longer, maybe I could have breakfast all
ready for them when they woke up.

"Ian?" Miz Pickens's head appeared at the hole
in the ceiling. "Don't you go filling your belly with
food this morning. Just a glass of milk, and that's
it. Anita and me, we'll be down directly."

"Yes, Miz Pickens." I was a little angry. Up to
now I'd been allowed to eat all I wanted of whatever food there was. The refrigerator was almost
full. Why set a limit on the day of the big party?

Then the answer came to me. We'd be having
some kind of special food later, and Miz Pickens
didn't want me stuffing myself with the regular
fare.

"Go take off your duds and put this on." Miz
Pickens tossed a ball of blue-denim cloth down
through the hole. "Just this and your old sneakers
and nothin' else. Understand?"

"Yes'm." I picked up the cloth and pulled it
straight. It was a worn, faded pair of blue jeans
that Dad had brought up in the suitcase. But Miz
Pickens had cut both legs off, leaving only what

amounted to a pair of shorts.

So that was it. We were going swimming. I was sure there'd be a pool or a stream somewhere nearby where we'd splash and paddle about and have lots of fun. And afterward there'd be food. Something really special.

But if it was to be a swimming party, why was I going to be the guest of honor?

By the time I'd changed into the shorts and my battered sneakers, Anita and her mother had come down out of the loft. They both ate hearty breakfasts, and I couldn't help feeling annoyed that all I was allowed was a glass of milk. I waited quietly while they finished and Anita rinsed the dishes in the sink. Then I got up from my stool.

"Okay," I said with grin. "Let's get started with the party. Lead me to the water."

"Water?" Miz Pickens screwed up her face and looked at me oddly. "What water?"

"You said we were going to have a party today. And with these cutoffs and not eating anything for breakfast, I just figured we were going swimming."

Miz Pickens shook her head. Again she and

Anita exchanged secret smiles. "It ain't that kind of a party, Ian."

"Then what . . . ?"

"Sit down a minute, and we'll talk. Me and Anita have had a lot of discussions about you while I was taking her to and from school. And we've come to a kind of decision about those wings of yours."

Uh-oh. So that was it. "You're planning on sending me back home," I said. "You don't want me here any longer. So it's a going-away party."

"Oh, pshaw, boy! We're not chasing you away."

I saw Anita grin with delight.

"Y'see, Ian, it's occurred to both of us that however those wings came to be, they weren't put on your back just to make your life a misery. Seems to us that, if possible, they ought to be put to some use."

"Use? What use?"

"What they were made for, of course."

It took me a moment to understand what Miz Pickens was getting at. "You . . . you mean . . ."

"That's right, Ian. Today we're going to have a flying party. And like I said, you're the guest of honor."

I shook my head. "It won't work."

"You never know until you try," said Anita.

"But I did try—while you were away," I told her. "I flapped my wings as hard as I could. Nothing happened."

"Hmmm." Miz Pickens thought about this for a moment. "Lad, you've been given wings nearly as big as tablecloths. You've lost a lot of weight, too, so you should rise off the ground easier. And the muscles of your back—the ones that make the wings flap—are strong and powerful. It seems to me that you are being made ready for something."

"Like flying? But I already told you—"

"Maybe the three of us can think of a way to make it work," said Anita. "After all, three heads are better than one."

"C'mon, Ian." Miz Pickens got up from her stool. "Let's go."

She and Anita headed for the cabin door. Reluctantly I followed along.

Outside, we walked a short distance from the cabin. "Okay," said Miz Pickens. "Now give those wings a try."

"I still don't think they'll—"

"Ian, you think too darned much!" Anita

snapped. "Stop trying to figure things out in your head and just do what Mama says."

I spread my wings wide. Anita and Miz Pickens stepped back. I began with a gentle flapping.

"Faster!" Miz Pickens ordered.

I beat the great wings harder and harder. The effort was something like rowing a boat against a swift current. Clouds of dust surrounded me, and I felt a gentle lifting sensation throughout my body. My feet, however, would not leave the ground.

Finally tired muscles in aching shoulders forced me to stop. I folded my wings against my body.

"That ain't working at all," said Miz Pickens. "I guess only them little songbirds can take flight from a standing start."

"Then can we go back inside?" I asked. "I'd like some more breakfast."

"Not just yet, Ian," Miz Pickens replied. "There's got to be something else we can try."

"You know," said Anita, "I saw a goose once down at Lake Tyrol. It was getting itself into the air. It kind of skittered along the lake like an airplane taking off from a runway. Finally its body came clear of the water, and for a while it looked like it was running on the surface. And all the time its wings were widespread. It finally got up into the air, but it had to go nearly the full width of the lake to do it."

"Hmmm." Miz Pickens rubbed her chin. "Mebbe you do need a running start, Ian."

"Do I have to? This is getting really silly."

"It's not silly," Anita said. "We're finding out what those wings are good for."

"Go over yonder, by the trees," Miz Pickens ordered. "When I shout, you come running this way, fast as you can. When you've got speed up, spread those wings out and pull up your feet."

"But what if the wings won't hold me up?"

"Then you'll fall. Haven't you ever had a tumble before?"

"Yes'm."

"Then you know it's nothing to be afraid of. Now git!"

I walked to the far edge of the clearing and turned, waiting for Miz Pickens's signal. "Go, Ian!" she cried out.

I ran toward her and Anita with my arms and legs pumping furiously. Then I spread my wings.

I could feel my body start to rise. There was no

great strain at my shoulder blades. Instead, the sensation was of being held in an invisible net that was gently lifting my whole body.

My heels left the ground, and I was running only on the tips of my toes. I was thrilled and frightened at the same time. Instinctively, I pulled the wings slightly closer to my body. I sank back down until my feet were flat on the ground again. When I reached Anita and her mother, I folded the wings against my back.

"I thought for a second there you were going to make it," Anita told me. "Why didn't you pull up your feet, Ian?"

"I . . . I was scared."

"Scared, huh?" snapped Miz Pickens. "Well you just try that again, Ian Carras. And if you don't lift your legs this time, I'll give you something to be really scared of!"

I took a minute to catch my breath. Then back I went to my starting point.

When I turned, I saw Anita where I'd left her. Miz Pickens was standing nearer. She seemed to be picking up something from the ground.

"You run to Anita, like you did last time," she said. "Never mind me. Go, Ian!"

I went. My legs moved up and down like a pair of pistons. When I felt I couldn't get another bit of speed from my straining body, I spread my wings wide.

At the same time something hard struck my ankle. It hurt. Still racing forward, I looked over at Miz Pickens.

She had a handful of stones. And she was throwing them at my feet, as fast as she could hurl them. Quickly I lifted my feet, just to keep from being struck again.

And I soared.

The wings supported me as I glided along. At first I curled my legs beneath me like those of a newborn baby. Then I found it was easier to stretch them out behind.

I was moving really fast. I stared down at the earth, which seemed to be rushing by as I hung in the air. Raising my head, I saw myself heading right at Anita.

Lifting the front edges of the wings, I brought myself to an upright position in the air. I slowed down, and my toes touched the ground. I began to run, but my feet couldn't keep up with the rest of my body. I plunged into Anita's outstretched arms, and we both tumbled to the ground.

I thought I might have hurt her. But she got up, helped me to my feet, and kissed my cheek with a loud smack.

"You did it, Ian!" she crowed. "You flew!"

I was dizzy with the success of the experiment. I wanted to sit down somewhere and just gloat over the experience. But Miz Pickens was having none of that.

"Now try it again," she said. "Just remember to lift your feet, for I'm not throwing any more stones."

After a running start, I glided a second time, with my arms folded against my chest and my legs stretched out behind. I did not, however, stop near Anita and her mother. Instead I crossed the full width of the clearing. As I drew near the trees, I tilted the wings slightly and turned. I felt my body lift.

Then it dropped—hard! It was a crash landing if there ever was one.

I picked myself up and saw Anita running toward me. "Ian, are you all right?" she exclaimed.

I rubbed my fingers against my chin, which had been scraped raw. "A few bumps," I said. "But I'm okay. I want to keep on practicing."

"We'll go in and rest awhile first," said Miz Pickens as she walked up to us. "And you get some food in you, Ian. I didn't allow you much breakfast, for I wanted to keep your weight down. But you can't keep on without nourishment."

We rested for perhaps half an hour. I sat on the porch, munching a sandwich and thinking of my next flight. In my mind I could almost picture how I'd have to move my wings to rise or turn or even land properly.

The wings—the wings I'd been so ashamed of. Except for them, I'd never have had the awesome experience of gliding through the air, held up by those things sprouting from my back. I spread them wide and peeked over my shoulder at the two great sails. I was . . . I was . . .

I was almost proud of them.

We went at it again. While the gliding was easy, flapping the wings to lift myself was very difficult. Gaining just a few feet of altitude required a tremendous amount of energy. After only a minute or so of straining, I had to land to relax the aching muscles in my back.

By midmorning I was getting pretty good at

gliding from one side of the clearing to the other, and even making turns. I was also getting far too cocky for my own good. While in flight I'd make swimming motions with my hands and feet or spread my arms and flutter my fingers as if they alone kept me in the air.

I decided to make one final flight before lunch. I launched myself into the air and zoomed past Miz Pickens and Anita. They waved at me as I passed. I looked back at them, loving their approving smiles.

I was still looking backward when their smiles changed to frightened surprise. Anita shouted something. I saw her lips move, but the sound never reached me. I glanced up ahead to select a place to land.

And what had frightened them terrified me.

My glide had carried me beyond the edge of the sheer cliff. Instead of having the ground a few feet beneath me, I was high up in the sky. Far below, the trees of the forest seemed like thousands of spears, all pointing right at me.

I was so scared, I forgot to keep my wings spread. They folded to my body. I dropped like a stone.

Frantically I pushed them wide again. The fall slowed. But by now I was halfway down the side of the cliff.

To my right was the bare rock wall of the mountainside. I looked everywhere for a safe place to land. There was none. Only trees, as far as I could see. If I crashed into them, every bone in my body would be broken. I was going to die, if I didn't do something quick. Yet even with my wings outstretched, I fell downward—always downward.

The branches of the trees seemed to move up at me like huge, grasping hands. I pumped my wings hard until I was hanging motionless in the air. But I couldn't keep it up for long. Soon I began to fall again.

I glided nearer to the cliff. Maybe, I thought, I could find a crack in the rock that I could hang on to until help came. Tilting my wings, I moved closer to the wall of stone. Closer.

And I made an amazing discovery.

The slight wind in the valley below had to move *up* when it reached the mountain. I could feel it against both my face and the undersides of my wings.

I began to rise—slowly at first, and then faster.

It just happened, with no effort from me.

I glided away from the rock face. The wind no longer helped me, and I settled downward.

Why, I could keep this up forever. Whenever I needed to rise upward, all I had to do was glide back near the mountain.

I decided to do a little exploring. First I let the wind take me all the way up to the top of the cliff. There were Anita and Miz Pickens. They called for me to come back to them. I waved and shouted that I was in no danger.

Then I glided outward. I wasn't afraid of the trees below anymore.

I spotted a small clearing in the forest. A farmer held the handles of a plow pulled by a mule. I made a couple of circles above them, and my shadow moved across the field of brown dirt. The farmer paid no attention.

Back to the cliff again for more height. Then I floated over a mountain that was bare and rocky and looked like a man's bald head.

That's when I made another discovery.

A current of warm air came up from the rock. It lifted me. I realized I didn't have to return to my cliff when I wanted to rise. All I needed was a place where there were no trees and the ground was heated by the sun.

I could stay in the sky for hours.

A little ribbon of road curved back and forth in a crooked valley, and cars that looked like bugs rolled along it. Ha, ha. The cars had to follow the road. I could go straight to anywhere I wanted, with just a slight movement of my wings.

A short way off I saw a hawk circling the tree-tops. I decided to go over and say hello. I could move without a sound, and got really close to the bird before it saw me. When it did, it gave a single squawk of surprise and fright, and dropped into the trees. I started laughing, forgot about keeping my wings straight, and almost tumbled out of the sky.

I wondered what all the people in Blanton would think if they could see me now. How would it be if I flew over that way and—

No. The reporters would still be there. And Dad and Mom would get even angrier than they were already. I was having fun. Why ruin it?

Finally, even though I was simply soaring, the muscles of my back started getting tired from holding the wings outstretched. I looked around, found the rock cliff, and glided toward it.

Anita and Miz Pickens were still waiting for me. I flew above them, circled, and came in for a landing.

My landings still left something to be desired, and when I fell out of the sky onto the hard ground, both knees and the palm of my left hand got skinned.

I didn't care. Miz Pickens helped me up and mussed my hair and told me how grand it was to see me floating in the sky. And Anita hugged me and said she was proud of me.

I wanted to fly again right away. But Miz Pickens said no. "We don't want you getting weary while you're up in the air," she said. "Just rest up, and you can fly again tomorrow."

That night, when I went to bed, I couldn't sleep. I just lay there on my stomach, imagining I was still gliding through the air above the mountains. I was like no other person who'd ever lived. Without machinery of any kind, I could fly.

I had wings!

8

The next morning—Sunday—I got up early, gob-
bled down a quick breakfast, and walked out of
the cabin to the edge of the great cliff. I could
hardly wait to try my wings again.

For a long time I stood there, staring down at
the trees far below. Sure, I knew I could fly. But
it was kind of scary to think of gliding out over
the edge. What if my wings no longer worked.
What if . . . ?

Finally I got up my courage. I walked back, ran
as hard as I could, spread my wings, and . . . I was
flying.

I soared beyond the cliff and then circled back,
catching the draft of wind. It lifted me, just as it
had done yesterday.

I was no longer afraid. After rising high above
the clearing, I tried a few tricks just to see what I
could do with my wings. I could swoop and turn,

but trickier movements were impossible, as I found out when I attempted a loop-the-loop and dropped far down toward the trees before I could untangle my wings and spread them to catch the air.

Next I tried hovering motionless, like the hawk I'd seen. I finally got the hang of it, and slight adjustments of my shoulders kept me from either rising or falling.

I pretended I was the hawk, searching for prey. I saw movement on a narrow trail through the woods. It was a dog, trotting along without a care in the world. I folded my wings and plunged downward. Just above the trees I began a long glide. When I was right over the dog, I screamed like an attacking bird.

The dog looked up. Then it gave a loud yip and scuttled off into the forest with its tail between its legs. Hey, this was really fun. Ian Carras, the bird man! Look out below!

Back at the cliff I caught the wind and rose up to the clearing. Miz Pickens stood there, waving to me. I landed and managed not to take a tumble.

"It's Sunday, Ian," she said. "Anita and me will be off to church soon. You'd best stay here and out

of sight. And there'll be no flying while we're
gone."

"But—"

"No buts. I'll not be worrying all through the
sermon about whether you've taken a tumble."

"No, ma'am."

"And from here on, the only times you'll fly is
when either Anita or me can be here to watch."

I wanted to argue. But there was a no-nonsense
look in Miz Pickens's eyes that made argument
impossible.

I flew Monday, with Miz Pickens looking on,
and again on Tuesday, when Anita got home from
school. "One flight per day will be plenty for the
present," Miz Pickens told me. "There's work to be
done around here, and I'll expect you to help with
it. Having wings is a rare and wonderful thing, Ian,
but you'd best learn right away that there's more
to life than playing like you're a bird."

Anita couldn't get enough of my adventures
when I told her about them in the evening.

"There's nothing I can't see when I'm up there,
Anita. It's all so . . . so . . ."

"Are you still feeling sorry for yourself on account of those wings, Ian?"

"No. No! When I'm flying, it's like I was more than just human. Like I was one of those Greek gods or something!"

She'd grin as if she were as pleased with my wings as I was. Sometimes she'd walk behind me as I sat on a stool and spread the wings out as wide as they would reach. Then she'd just look at them for five or ten minutes.

Because of the reporters, I'd kept well away from the skies above Blanton. But on Wednesday I was seen by people for the first time.

I was gliding just a little ways above the road that ran through the valley. Suddenly a car came around a curve heading in my direction. All at once the car skidded to a stop. A man got out, shouted something through the window, and pointed at me.

The other car doors opened. A woman and two children popped out. The whole family stared at me like I was a creature from Mars.

Maybe they thought I was!

I flew away as fast as I could. It took quite a while, however, to soar over the mountains and out of sight.

That afternoon Dad called.

"Dad, my wings . . . I flew!" I said joyfully.

"I know, Ian," he said mournfully. "So does everybody within a hundred miles."

"Oh, Dad! It was . . . it was . . . But how did you know?"

"You were seen by some tourists. Right now they're down at the hotel, with every reporter in town interviewing them. Tomorrow morning the story'll be in all the papers. With artists' sketches and everything. Oh, lord! Why me?"

"I don't really care about the reporters, Dad."

"Well *I* care!" Dad roared. "Sure, it's easy for you to ignore them, perched up on that mountain. But just try living here in Blanton for a few days and not being able to set foot outside the door without a police escort. I don't think you've got any idea what your mother and sister and I have been going through."

"If the reporters are bugging you, why don't you just go off somewhere and get away from them?"

"I'm running for mayor, for Pete's sake! I can't disappear at a time like this."

"Then you'll just have to put up with the reporters."

I heard Dad groan loudly. "I'll have a talk with Donovan," he said, "and tell him to get moving on finding a doctor to cut off those—"

"I . . . I really don't know if I want to lose my wings, Dad."

"How can you—"

"Dad, I flew. I *flew!*"

"Sure, sure," he replied impatiently. "But those wings won't do you a bit of good in the real world. Oh, you might end up in a freak show, but that's about it."

"I'm not a freak!" I screamed. "I'm just . . . different."

"I'll get back to you after I've seen Dr. Donovan," said Dad. "You and I will have a little talk—face to face."

Before I could reply, he hung up.

The next two days brought rain and brisk winds to the mountaintop. I didn't fly. I couldn't work outside. I just moped about the little cabin, getting in Miz Pickens's way and worrying about losing my magnificent wings.

On Friday evening the rain stopped, although the clouds were still low and threatening. I was just putting away the supper dishes when I heard a car drive into the clearing and pull up beside the cabin.

It was Dad. Mom was with him. Miz Pickens

opened the door and invited them inside.

"Getting up here was no fun," said Dad as Mom sat down in the rocking chair, "The road's a sea of mud. But we've got some great news, Ian. Dr. Donovan's located a surgeon who's going to do the operation."

"You mean to . . . to cut off my wings?"

"Of course. Isn't that what we've been planning for all this time?"

"But I already told you. I'm not sure that's what I want."

"What? I thought you'd be jumping for joy. Hey, weren't you just kidding when you talked about keeping—"

Suddenly he was interrupted by Miz Pickens. "Mr. Carras," she said, "I think it'd be best if Anita and me took a little walk. That way you can discuss your . . . uh . . . family matters without us listening in."

"But I don't want you to—" I began.

"No, Ian," said Anita. "Mama's right. This is between you and your folks. You have to settle it one way or the other without us butting in."

Without another word, they walked out of the cabin.

"Thank heaven they're gone," said Dad. "Maybe, Ian, living up here with that woman and her six-fingered girl has done something to your mind. I mean, when it comes to those wings . . ."

"Anita and Miz Pickens have been good to me, Dad. So don't start bad-mouthing them."

"Okay, okay," he said impatiently. "But the wings. Do you mean that after all the grief they've caused, you want to *keep* them?"

"I can fly, Dad. When I'm alone up there in the sky, I feel like . . . well, it's something neither you nor Mom nor Diane will ever understand. But—"

"Yeah, sure. Only you can't spend your whole life zooming around like a bird. And what happens when you come down on the ground? You'll stand out wherever you go, like a canary at a gathering of cats. Oh, I can hear it now: 'There goes Ian Carras. Yeah, that's right, the one with the wings.' A job? Forget it. The only place you'd work would be in a freak show."

"Don't say that word, Dad. It makes me mad."

"Oh, you don't like me saying 'freak,' huh? Well, I'm trying to get elected mayor, and I've got a son who's—"

"Is being elected the only thing—"

Dad went on as if he hadn't heard me.

"—a freak. A freak! A—"

"Lester, stop it! Stop it, I say!" Mom's scream echoed in the little cabin.

I'd never seen her defy Dad before, even in the smallest thing. Dad glared at her. "You keep out of this, Madeline."

"I won't! My family's tearing itself apart. It's time Ian heard about you and my father. You promised me you'd tell him, Lester."

"Grandpa Edwin?" I looked from Mom to Dad, puzzled. "Why bring him up?"

"Tell him, Lester," Mom repeated.

For a long time, Dad just stared at the floor. "When . . . when your mother and I were first married," he said finally, "my dream was to study law."

"Then why didn't you?" I asked.

"Because Grandpa Edwin was worried that I'd never be able to make enough money here in Blanton to care for his daughter—my wife," he replied bitterly. "So Grandpa Edwin got me my first job—as a teller at the bank. Then Grandpa Edwin arranged for me to be appointed loan manager. After that, Grandpa Edwin made me an account executive. Finally, just before he died, Grandpa Edwin saw to it that I became bank president. How I hated that man!"

"But Dad—if he gave you all those things . . ."

"That's the whole point. He *gave* me everything. I never achieved anything by myself."

Dad fell silent. My wings felt heavy upon my back. I had flown. I knew the glory of having control of my own life—a thing my father was still striving for.

"Running for mayor," Dad went on at last, "is the first time I've ever had the guts to try for something on my own. And I'd have won. I'm sure of it. But now—"

He strode toward the door. "Now, Ian, you can have a big laugh about how your old man is feeling sorry for himself. But I don't have to hang around in here to listen to it."

He stomped out onto the porch. The door slammed loudly behind him.

Neither Mom nor I laughed. We both looked first at the closed door and then at one another.

"Ian," said Mom in little more than a whisper. "Now you know why Dad hates your wings so— and why you've got to have them removed."

"I don't *have* to do anything," I replied. "But as long as family secrets are being brought out in the open, I want to ask you something."

"Me? But what . . ."

"Mom, ever since I can remember, Diane's been getting all the pats on the back from you and Dad, and I've had my nose rubbed in the dirt. How come? What makes Diane so special and me such a nerd?"

"Whatever do you mean?" Mom glanced about the cabin as if she didn't want to look me in the eye. "We're equally proud of both our children."

"Come on! You know better than that. What's Miss Perfect Princess got going for her that I haven't?"

I saw tears glisten in my mother's eyes. "Must we discuss this now? I'd much rather talk about what's going to happen to your wings."

"Either we talk about it or I won't even consider having the operation."

Mom pulled a handkerchief from her purse. "You can really be cruel when you want to, Ian Carras."

"If I'm cruel, you and Dad are the ones who taught me how. Now I want to know why."

The handkerchief disappeared inside her purse. "Very well. But in my opinion you're far too young to understand."

"I've done a lot of growing up in the past months, Mom."

"Af—after your father and I were married, we wanted to start a family right away. But for more than two years—nothing. We were desperately unhappy."

"Then Diane came along, huh?"

"Yes. We've told you about her birth."

"Sure. She was a preemie. But now she's okay, so everything's fine."

"Well it wasn't fine back then! Diane was born five weeks early, and she weighed less than three pounds. She had to remain in the hospital for a long time, and Dad and I never could be sure from one day to the next whether she would be alive or dead. Our first child! We were almost insane with worry.

"Even when she was allowed to come home, she needed constant care. Feeding every hour or two, around the clock. A tank of oxygen always ready at her bedside. Wrapping her in blankets and then removing them and sponging her with water, so she never became too cold or too warm. And always the concern that she might just stop breathing or that there might be some brain damage. Two years of worry and almost no sleep and never-ending care. And then . . ."

"And then what?"

"Just when we thought she was developing into a fine, healthy baby, she began having problems in her lungs."

"Problems?"

"Oh, the doctors had a long name for it. Very simply, her lungs were weak and sensitive. She was allergic to everything. All our rugs had to be removed, and I was constantly mopping to pick up dust. We threw out all her stuffed toys, and I couldn't even use perfumes or hair sprays.

"Diane caught colds one after another, and each time she had to be in the hospital. Even when she was home, she always needed to be looked after. We wondered if she'd ever get well and be just a normal child. There were times during your sister's first six years when I'd gladly have paid a million dollars for just a few hours of uninterrupted sleep."

"Six years, huh? So in the middle of all this, I got born."

Mom nodded. "You were healthy, right from the first. But still, you needed feeding and changing and being taken for walks and all the other things a baby requires. And . . . and . . ."

All at once Mom opened her mouth, and a great moan, like a scream for help, came forth. Then she covered her face with her hands and her body shook.

"I resented you, Ian. So did Dad. We resented every minute you took away from caring for Diane. Sure, the doctor told us to hire help. But we thought that would be like admitting we'd failed as parents. So we just—somehow—kept on."

"But I don't remember—"

"Oh, you were far too young. Finally, of course, Diane rallied and began to develop like any other girl. But by then we were in the habit of treating her like someone special. She'd turned into a beautiful girl. She did well in school and had lots of friends. All the things we wanted for our first child."

"And me?" I asked.

"You never demanded attention, Ian. You never seemed to *need* us."

I felt tears start in my own eyes. "I . . . I needed you," I said. "But you were never there for me. It was always Diane, Diane, Diane!"

"I'm sorry. I'm so sorry for what we've done to you. But from now on, I promise, Dad and I will do whatever we can make it better. If . . . if only you'll give us the chance. Once those wings are gone, we'll all—"

"No, Mom," I replied.

"You . . . you're not going to have them removed?" she gasped.

"That's not what I meant. It's just— Mom, whatever I decide about my wings, it won't be because of how Grandpa Edwin treated Dad or how things were when I was a baby. Can't you understand that?"

"Please, Ian," she pleaded.

I shook my head. "I have to figure out what I want."

I got up and walked to the cabin door.

"Where are you going, Ian?"

"Outside. I've got some thinking to do—by myself."

"Don't go!" she cried out. "We can . . ."

The door slammed shut behind me. Dad was seated on the edge of the porch with his head bowed. He didn't look up at me as I walked by.

I didn't say a word to him.

I went down the steps and into the night.

I seated myself on a rock in the middle of the clearing. Overhead, the stars were a million tiny holes punched in the great black blanket of sky. My wings fanned the still air.

"Ian, is that you?"

Anita's voice came from out of the darkness.

"Yes."

"Are you all right? D'you want to talk or . . . or . . ."

"No, Anita. I have to be alone." Mom and Dad couldn't help me make my choice. Neither could Miz Pickens or Anita. It was up to me to decide, all by myself.

Until now, choosing had always been so easy. Go to the movies or do my homework? Spend my allowance on candy and fun, or save for a new baseball glove? Wear old, scuzzy clothes to school or put on something really sharp?

Even when I picked wrong, it was no big deal. Homework could be made up, and the baseball glove could wait a few weeks, and clothes could be changed.

But my wings?

If my wings were removed by the doctor, I'd no longer be a . . . a "freak" who was laughed at and pointed to and chased by reporters. I could go back home, where things might be better, as Mom had promised. After a while everybody'd forget about the wings, and I'd be just like everybody else.

But . . .

Never to fly again—never to experience the rush of wind across my great wings. Never to look down at the world from on high and know that no other person throughout history had ever done such a thing. To give up the one aspect of my body that made me special and unique and that filled my life with wonder and awe.

Whichever way I went, there would be sadness and a sense of loss. Was this a part of growing up—the agony of making such choices?

If so, I wanted to stay a child forever.

Alone and afraid, I sat there in the darkness.

9

When I said good-bye to them on the mountain, Miz Pickens hugged me tightly and Anita kissed my cheek. I managed to get into the backseat of the car, kneel, and slam the door before I began blubbering like a baby.

Not a word was spoken by either Mom or Dad as we came down off the mountain.

We drove for nearly an hour until we came to a tiny airport. Leaving the car there, we got into a small plane. It was a tight fit for me and my wings, but finally I wriggled through the plane's door and lay facedown across two of the passenger seats.

The engine roared, and the plane lurched into the air. It took us hundreds of miles from Blanton.

Just before we landed, I peered through the plane window, and I saw the lights of a great city below us. From the airport, a taxi brought us to a big redbrick building.

During the next two days I lay on my stomach

in a high bed. I was examined and X-rayed. Blood was sucked from my arm with a needle. There were pills to swallow, and I had to answer endless questions about how I was feeling. A lot of doctors kept coming into my room to stretch out my wings and see what they looked like.

Once, a reporter tried to break in. A guard outside the door stopped him. I could hear loud shouting coming from the hallway.

On the morning of the third day, I was wheeled on a table into a big room with white tile on the walls. Several people in white, with masks tied over their noses and mouths, gathered around the table. A woman held a rubber cup with a black hose attached to it. She put the cup to my face.

"Just breathe deeply," she told me, "and count backward from one hundred."

"One hundred ... ninety-nine ... ninety-eight ... ninety-six . . . ninety-three . . ."

I don't remember anything more.

When I came to, I was groggy, as if my brain had turned into cotton. My eyelids felt heavy and I kept them closed. It was hard for me to figure out whether I was really awake or still sleeping.

I was back in bed, lying on my stomach and held that way by padded straps wrapped about my wrists and attached to the railings of the hospital bed.

I heard a voice. It sounded like Dad, whispering something to Mom.

A dull pain throbbed across my back. I twitched my shoulder blades under their thick wrapping of bandages and dressing.

My wings were gone. Never again would I soar and glide and split the wind and know the glorious feeling of being closer to heaven than any other mortal who had ever lived.

I felt a hand grip mine. All at once, for the first time since the wings had begun to grow upon my back, I felt at ease and at peace with myself.

I knew that in future days and years I'd have doubts about the choice I had made. There would be sadness over the loss of my great wings—a sense that I was trapped upon the surface of the earth instead of able to fly high above it. And maybe the long and bitter arguments with my parents would continue, and it might be difficult or even impossible to regain the friendship of Wayde Flack.

But I would never be alone with my thoughts and misgivings . . . and my grief. For on the hand that gently gripped mine were six fingers.